UNFAMILIAR TERRITORY

A LOWESTOFT CHRONICLE ANTHOLOGY

Books in the Lowestoft Chronicle Anthology Series

Lowestoft Chronicle 2011 Anthology
Far-Flung and Foreign
Intrepid Travelers
Somewhere, Sometime
Other Places
Grand Departures
Invigorating Passages
Steadfast Trekkers
The Vicarious Traveler
An Adventurous Spirit
A Place to Pause

"Full of great talent and exceptionally well written pieces. An entertaining read."
—Tara Smith, *The Review Review*

"*Lowestoft Chronicle* is a wonderful new addition to the world of creative writing."
—Tony Perrottet, acclaimed author of *The Naked Olympics*

"Reading *Lowestoft Chronicle* is like jostling through a sprawling bazaar in Tashkent or Ulaanbaatar, with eyes wide open and wits on high alert. Invigorating, too."
—Victor Robert Lee, author of *Performance Anomalies*

"A standout among a growing universe of online journals. Every issue delivers a cornucopia of entertaining and thought-provoking stories and articles."
—Michael C. Keith, acclaimed author of *The Next Better Place*

"A brilliant, savory, sharp, amusing and varied taste of my favorite magazine, *Lowestoft Chronicle*. I'm delighted that a place exists for this kind of travel writing. Nicholas Litchfield has put together something very special, something to celebrate, enjoy, savor."
—Jay Parini, bestselling author of *The Last Station* and *The Passages of H.M.*

"The *Lowestoft Chronicle* is both classy and fun to read. A work accomplished by careful attention to detail and quality."
—Sheldon Russell, Spur Award-winning author of *A Forgotten Evil*

"Terrific anthology. The writing here is fresh, surprising, and alive. If you aren't familiar with *Lowestoft Chronicle*, head on over there. They publish, on a consistent basis, excellent fiction, poetry, and non-fiction."
—Nicholas Rombes, acclaimed author of
A Cultural Dictionary of Punk, 1974-1982

"*Lowestoft Chronicle* publishes some of the finest work of travel writing on the Internet today."   —Krystal Sierra, *The Review Review* (5-Star Review)

"This is the only literary magazine I read these days, and it's always enjoyable. It takes the reader to a wide variety of literary destinations, and makes even a confirmed hermit like me want to get up and go somewhere. Highly recommended."   —James Reasoner, *New York Times* bestselling author

"Charm, love of travel, often sly humor, and a clear reverance of story make up the backbone of *Lowestoft Chronicle*."

—Keith Rosson, acclaimed author of *Fever House* and *The Devil by Name*

"Editor Nicholas Litchfield has once again done admirable work in selecting and presenting a memorable miscelleny of fiction, nonfiction, and verse that beckons to literary travelers and leads them onward from one entertaining stop to the next." —Timothy J. Lockhart, author of *Smith* and *Pirates*

"Nicholas Litchfield's selection of stories, poems, memoirs and interviews is a treasure for readers who enjoy a good dose of humor with their armchair travel."

—Mary Donaldson-Evans, author of *Madame Bovary at the Movies*

"The much-admired *Lowestoft Chronicle* [is] an eclectic and innovative online journal. Packed into the pages are stories to entice, enthral, and entertain… incisive and enlightening interviews…[and] a tasty blend of pleasing and deftly prepared poems." —Pam Norfolk, *Lancashire Post*

"How did I not know about the *Lowestoft Chronicle*? If you're late to this travel and literary parade as well, check out Nicholas Litchfield's superb online journal specializing in all things to do with travel, literature, and the overlap between these life-nourishing activities.

—James R. Benn, acclaimed author of the Billy Boyle mystery series

"A refreshingly original collection of sharp tales. Overall, it's entertaining, varied, and clever writing." —*Kirkus Reviews*

"The literary equivalent of Rick's Café in *Casablanca*, where travelers of all stripes pull up a stool and swap stories at the bar. Handsomely designed and expertly curated, *Lowestoft Chronicle* drives us into the arms of experience."

—Scott Dominic Carpenter, author of *Theory of Remainders*

"A fun read." —*New York Journal of Books*

"In this quarterly, you'll find creative nonfiction, short stories, and a few poems, with a welcome dose of humor in many. Wander around the site and you'll find intriguing stories." —Pat Tompkins, Afar.com

"A fantastic online literary magazine that mixes humour and travel. There's lots of good fiction there." —Allister Timms, author of *The Killing Moon*

"*Lowestoft Chronicle* is contemporary and worldly but with a sepia charm. It's a Baedeker for the vicarious traveler in the age of globalization."
—Ivy Goodman, acclaimed author of *Heart Failure*

"A solid collection of funny and fine travel-themed stories, poetry, essays and interviews that easily fits in a back pocket or carry-on bag."
—Frank Mundo, Examiner.com

"Three attributes of a good literary journal are variety, quality, and the unexpected. *Lowestoft Chronicle* supplies all three."
—Robert Wexelblatt, award-winning author of *Zublinka Among Women*

"I'm always impressed with the quarterly online literary magazine, *Lowestoft Chronicle*—it's filled with intriguing fiction, non-fiction, poetry, and interviews. Click on over for good reading."
—Matthew P. Mayo, Spur Award-winning author of *Tucker's Reckoning*

"It's unique and the quality of the writing is amazingly high...both provocative and enjoyable. Highest praise: it made me want to write short stories again."
—Luke Rhinehart, internationally bestselling author of *The Dice Man*

"A delightful blend of captivating stories that inspired me to step away from my desk and experience all the vast glories beyond the screen."
—Brian Sacca, actor and screenwriter of *Buffaloed*

"Fresh, original, unpretentious...a pure delight."
—Jim Daniels, award-winning author of *Places/Everyone* and *Birth Marks*

"Reading the *Lowestoft Chronicle* is like looking at a Norman Rockwell painting."
—Christopher Cosmos, bestselling author of *Once We Were Here*

"This cornucopia of riveting tales and vivid poetry...abounds with amazing language, arresting insight, and sharply drawn landscapes."
—Linda Boroff, screenwriter of *Murder in Fashion*

UNFAMILIAR TERRITORY

A LOWESTOFT CHRONICLE ANTHOLOGY

EDITED BY NICHOLAS LITCHFIELD

FOREWORD BY MARK JACOBS

Lowestof
Chronicl
Press

UNFAMILIAR TERRITORY

SUBMISSIONS

The editors welcome submissions of poetry and prose. For submission information please visit our website at www.lowestoftchronicle.com or email: submissions@lowestoftchronicle.com

Published by Lowestoft Chronicle Press, Cambridge, Massachusetts
www.lowestoftchronicle.com

First edition: January 2025

Cover and book design by Nicholas Litchfield
Art credits include: iStockphoto.com/CSA Images

ISBN 13: 978-1-7323328-4-3
ISBN 10: 1-7323328-4-3

Library of Congress Control Number: 2024930537

Printed in the United States of America

CONTENTS

CREATIVE NON-FICTION

FOREWORD

Mark Jacobs

What is it about unfamiliar territory that draws us? The age-old answer has to do with the pull of the new, a hunger for the unknown. Over time, in our life of habit, we become impatient with the familiar. We are fed up with the commonplace. Routine drives us crazy. The stability we once craved inexplicably now feels like a drag. We want to move, and keep moving. 'Exotic' did not used to be a term of opprobrium. The adventurous of spirit find themselves on the road. But they have company: those who travel not by choice but out of necessity. Exiles and the dispossessed, people who can't make a living where they were born, or can't find peace. And there are a certain number of individuals who simply want more, want different. For all of them, the allure of unfamiliar territory has to do with possibility. They might get lucky.

This is the way human history seems to have been, and today, no fundamental change threatens the pattern. People still travel the globe for all the reasons listed above. These days, however, there may be another driver. Call it the digital imperative. Digitalization seeps into just about every crack and corner of our existence. Someone is always, *always*, trying to sell us something that technology has only now made possible. We are relentlessly plied with offers of one or another brand of virtual reality, an experience that is superior to the analog original. We are promised intensified perception, and increased efficiency. New and improved is newer now, and still more improved.

The digital world spreads out before us like a boundless lake. It's so vast, it's too big to comprehend, let alone measure. The water shimmers invitingly. Its colors mesmerize the eye. And it comes with a soundtrack. The quality of the audio keeps pace with the ever-improving visual show. This lake gets bigger every day. We are told, and we are inclined to believe, that it will keep getting bigger into an unforeseeable future.

Enormous as it is, though, this lake is scarcely an inch deep.

If we're lucky, we realize just how shallow it is. If we're lucky, when we realize it, we turn away. We go back to what still goes by the archaic name of 'the real world.' Once we're back on terra firma, we look around. We stretch, and recover our senses. The dirt beneath our feet pulses with insect life. The oak tree in the front yard bears a black scar from a bolt of lightning; how many years ago was that? Next door, in the neighbor's driveway, sits an old red Chevy with a crumpled fender. There was an accident, not fatal, but there's a story behind it that wants to be told. Regrounding ourselves, we find that all these things look better than we remember. They reclaim our attention. They captivate us, entertain us, stimulate us.

You can't see all there is to see in this reclaimed real world all at once. There is too much to take in. But it's waiting: over a hill; down a highway that glistens, receding to a horizon; across town, following crazyquilt streets that baffle the best sense of direction. The eye and the imagination are happily seduced by distance, which can sometimes be discovered close at hand.

The selections in this anthology invite us to grab a map, follow a trail, get lost and, possibly, found again. They encourage us to take a break along the way, have a cold drink, consult fellow travelers about the road conditions ahead. Spend the night somewhere sketchy. Feel the pea underneath a heap of mattresses. Listen hard for the spinning of a secret wheel; it produces silver thread of incalculable value. Keep an eye out for wild animals, rare birds, brigands, shamans, con men, saints in disguise. These poems and essays and stories promise to take us to the unfamiliar territory our best selves crave. The great thing is, they deliver.

A MÉLANGE OF THE STRANGE AND UNEXPECTED

Nicholas Litchfield

"The writing is skilled, the choices rich, the passages manifold, and the invigoration unfailing"

— Robert Wexelblatt, author of *Zublinka Among Women*

Robert Wexelblatt's fiction has been described as "loaded with wit, bristling with irony, draped in erudition and studded with metaphysics," and though this sounds like something our old proofreader may have hiccupped while searching the copy editor's desk for a bottle of Château Margaux, this was the shrewd determination of a *New York Times* book critic. Some time ago, the prolific Wexelblatt, a contributor to over 750 publications, gave this lucid evaluation of one of our collections: "An anthology of travel writing—generously conceived, like this one—should serve up a variety of trips to surprise and stimulate the mental traveler. Here you will find journeys not only to varied locales in space and time but into the inexhaustible intricacies of human psychology, adventures of all sorts and in every genre: poetry, nonfiction, stories."

I like to think that this valuation holds true with *Unfamiliar Territory*, the twelfth volume in our mixed-form anthology series. Encapsulated in this tome of colorful, global literature are works that survey the spectrum of emotion, offering, among other things, inspiration, caution, enlightenment, provocation, and invigoration. It's a place where you can find groves of diverting fiction—chiefly literary but which regularly embraces a diverse hue of styles. Narratives that lead you to joyful, forlorn, sinister, murky outcrops.

In stealthy, offbeat yarns like "P.C.T. - Please Call Them," where the death of a long-haul hiker in California spurs a seasoned park ranger to investigate the victim's shadowy past, David Hagerty expertly guides the reader off the marked trail and deep into the austere unknown. In contrast, in Barbara Bottner's enchanting family drama "Love More," a woman's "father issues" resurface as she prepares to bury her mother's ashes.

Again, father issues play a part in "The Pioneer Hotel," Elizabeth Sowden's vivid 1950s tale of a daughter's fraught relationship with her dipsomaniac father. You can practically hear the rats scooting across the creaky floorboards and taste the aroma of sweat and baccy and grief. Flashes of optimism and personal triumph on Wrigley Field offset the abiding sadness.

Steve Slavin's tongue-in-cheek Caribbean tale "The Island that Time Forgot" also projects a sense of personal achievement. The resourceful central character, a scruffy, loaferish university student, doesn't just land a cushy position in an island paradise but also has a neat little brush with fame.

Elsewhere, a factory employee reevaluates his future while collecting his colleague from prison during a challenging business trip between Southern California and Mexico in Jeff Burt's evocative "Mirage," and in Diana Senechal's masterfully reflective story "Volta," a woman draws poetic inspiration from a letter and reexamines a lost long-ago friendship. And while love loses its clarity in Charles Holdefer's humorous "Espèce de Cowboy," where an American ex-pat struggles to adapt, a middle-aged couple's marriage is strengthened while foraging for mushrooms in southeastern France in Jim Daniels' canny "Appropriate Distance."

Delve a little deeper into the collection, and you'll come across a fleet of stirring seafaring adventures. In "A Ship of Dreams," Kathy Dunkerley drolly explores sufferance in Miami, Florida, as a Disney Cruise saps a mother's desire to satisfy the whims of her daughter. Recklessness and retribution arise in Mark Jacobs' enthralling "Two Days Out From San Juan," where a resilient crewman must chart a very different course home. And fear and discontent lead a prudish English inventor to conceive a fast passage away from the economic and cultural hub of the East in James Gallant's amusing "An Englishman in Constantinople."

The witty and enlightening essay "It's a Crossing, Not a Cruise" continues the nautical theme. Here, Bill Brown details his experiences venturing from the UK to the USA by sea, relishing the quirky customs aboard a luxurious British transatlantic ocean liner.

Other travel-infused nonfiction pieces include Lorraine Caputo's revealing "The Mérida Express," in which the daring traveler, confined to a bustling passenger railcar for more than forty hours, starts to question the soundness of her decision to ride the express train from Mexico City to Mérida. In the charming "Don't Blink or You'll Miss It," Mary Kreienkamp recalls childhood family vacations and a father's steadfast desire to uphold their rigid itinerary. In "Rock Stars Come to St. Ingbert," C.B. Heinemann's buoyant recollections of life on the music circuit, a famous rock group gatecrashes a touring band's gig at a tiny venue in southwestern Germany. And in Jane Elkin's delightfully shocking "Cowlateral Damage," American tourists find themselves fleeing for their lives in Switzerland as a quaint Alpine festival gets out of control.

K.C. Wolfe leads off the Knights of the Road tales with "The Forest of Signs," his captivating account of an epic drive across North America, in which a quirky Canadian roadside attraction on the Alaska Highway in Yukon provides a young couple with vital respite and redirection. In the fascinating "The National Road," Tim Morris journeys along the nation's first federally funded interstate highway, documenting historical footnotes, markers, monuments, and the inevitable wrong turn. Adam Berlin's concise travelogue "but not The Scream" offers a tantalizing snapshot of the majestic beauty residing in villages throughout Norway, unimpeded by gaggles of tourists clamoring for the same selfie. And the stress of purchasing a car is taken up a few notches in "The Middle of Catskill-Nowhere," Katie Baker's tense memoir recounting her experiences with a private seller during the pandemic.

Interspersed between fiction and nonfiction are sometimes traditional and sometimes improvisatory poems with organic rhythms, unwilling to yield to conformity. These pulsating verses reflect on shifting landscapes, community struggles, inattentiveness, neglect, and pitiable public displays.

Ann Howells' "Goodbye to Dallas" and "San Antonio on My Birthday" offer wry observations on the coming and goings of the standpat and the progressive and the changing times in Texas. George Moore presents illuminating examinations of war and the abiding scars scorched into neighborhoods as disaster strikes in the stirring "Lights in Mexico" and "The Fires." Lee Clark Zumpe's "foreclosure" and "the ligustrum needs pruning" are emotive portraits of abandonment and the need for extra care and devotion. In contrast, extreme passion grips the seething homeowner in Robert Beveridge's "Chile Paste," an entertaining account of crime and punishment, with the tamer "Like Bats" presenting a breezy report of stormy times in Italy. And William Miller contemplates budding love in the buoyant "The Complete Poems of John Keats" and festering misery in his enjoyably provocative "Lady Macbeth."

This volume also includes interviews with *Lowestoft Chronicle* contributors Jim Daniels and Adam Berlin. Jim Daniels' stories and poems have garnered a slew of impressive accolades over the years. In fact, somewhere in America, there's a racecar sporting lines from one of his poems on its rooftop. In this interview, he discusses his newest chapbook, some of the tales in his most recent story collection, and his landmark first full-length book of poetry.

Despite early success that included film rights and high praise in periodicals like the *New York Times*, prizewinning novelist Adam Berlin didn't find the sort of fame his subsequent work merited. This interview examines his early work, the influence of his first literary agent, and his recent first story collection.

As many fine writers can attest, the hard graft required to market one's name, showcase one's talent, and profit from glowing endorsements is a familiar challenge. Like a vacation, there are the highs, and there are lows, and there are those moments—usually when the bill arrives—when we don't quite know what of make of things. Life suddenly becomes a series of unexpected, topsy-turvy moments that test our resolve and make us take a different look, perhaps crane our neck to see if we're on an episode of the hidden camera reality show *Candid Camera*.

Unfamiliar Territory is one of those moments. An intriguing mélange of the strange and unexpected. A poke in the rear that pilots the reader to unfamiliar, thought-provoking territory.

Relax, unclench, and savor the novel experience.

MIRAGE

Jeff Burt

I had traveled to Orange County by air and then drove I-5 and I-8 to Calexico to see Gabriel Trevino discharged from a drunk and disorderly because he would not stop shout-singing poems of Flores, of two men who love the same woman. It was Tuesday, and he'd been in jail since Sunday night.

"I had barely a drop to drink," he told me. "The words were intoxicated, such gloom as if night had drawn early on the day, but here in the flat of the valley, without mountains, the day never ends. Flores wrote about the soul, knowing it does not exist, but perhaps it only exists when there is longing, the frustration of desire.

That is the desert. That is why I sang the poems so loudly so that the mountains that ring this valley could hear how much the people ache."

"For that, they put you in jail," I asked.

"What could be more startling," Gabriel said, "than hearing the desert floor itself, the place of no life, speaking to the rest of existence?"

I paid Gabby's drunk and disorderly fine and took him to a motel. He slept three hours, then wanted to leave.

Gabriel worked as the national manager for a maquiladora in Mexicali, just across the border from Calexico, in the Sonoran Desert. Mexicali is home to over seven hundred and fifty thousand people, Calexico about forty thousand. Mexicali has many great Chinese restaurants, a few classy hotels, and a throbbing nightlife. The most frequented spot in Calexico is a Walmart.

Gabriel, or Gabby as he was called for his incessant fast-paced speech, owned a modest ranch near the canal that brought water from Calexico into Mexicali. He had planted fruit trees that could survive the hot summer provided the water ran, which he had insured by attaching his grandfather's water rights to the property. He also had a listless bull, a terrorizing burro, and a few dozen goats, which he had penned with twelve-foot fences after he had seen the goats stacked three tall trying to leap over the fence. Their primary purpose was for barbeque. He sold many each year to his neighbors for parties and celebrations.

I took Gabby across the border toward Mexicali, past a youth group encampment and a flock of young people working at the homes of old women, cleaning, fixing the walls so dirt did not seep through, and two repatching a roof on a shack that had several orange barrels in it. We turned east toward Yuma, following the sparkling water of the canal to Gabby's ranch.

"This is the oasis of the desert here," Gabby said. "To the west, you have the boulders of the Laguna Mountains and the rocks of the Cleveland Forest. It is not much to speak of and even less to see. To the east, you have the desert, all the way to Yuma. It is not much to see and even less to speak of. To the north, the desert, perhaps populated along the canals and a single golf course stealing water from the mouths of children and the roots of plants. To the south, there is nothing to speak of and nothing to see. The land is idle, lazy, produces nothing, and the only people who live there are those that can survive on nothing.

That is where my mother was born. My father came from the Sonora Mountains, a family of hard work, industry, producers, farmers, ranchers, and grove owners. It is from my father that I learned of the fruits of work. It is from my father that I learned the poetry of Flores. It was from my father that I learned to drink. All things that I am I trace to my father."

Gabby had an odd attachment to his father, who had been dead for nineteen years. Gabby believed in ancestor worship and attended séance-like sessions with a shaman to communicate with his father, but he had been unsuccessful. Stoked with psychedelic drugs, heated to a fever in the tent beyond what animals would tolerate, sucking smoke into his lungs, Gabby failed, the shaman told him, because he would not let go of things that bound him, his property, his work, even his wife, who participated in the sessions. More of Gabby's money went to the shaman for the sessions until he had only his job and his ranch left, no other assets. He had sold his car. He had even begun selling the goats to his neighbors rather than gifting them. His wife, who the shaman said had communicated with her grandmother, left him for the shaman, and shortly after, his wife and the shaman left for La Paz.

Gabby had a rift with his father shortly before his father died. He had plunged into the burgeoning electronics field, which his father considered a fad, and Gabby had married a woman with a sketchy past from the Pacific Coast, having been jailed several times for grifting. When Lupita became pregnant, Gabby's father refused to come down from his mountain ranch and visit. When Lupita miscarried, Gabby blamed his father, and back and forth the barbs flew, digging into each other like two roosters in a small pen with spurs attached to their feet.

Then, silence.

It was that silence Gabby was trying to crack and that brought him finally to alcohol, both daily and binging on weekends.

I had a friend in Rosarito who said we could use his villa on the weekend, and I thought it would be a good place for Gabby to start rehab.

We took Gabby's car, a 1966 white Thunderbird with modified shocks that made it feel like it was swimming on the road, never just a straight-ahead plowing through the air, but a slicing, a knifing, the car rolling over the air rather than the road. Soon after we left Mexicali, heading west on Highway 2 with the sun reddening our necks and the left side of our faces, the traffic slowed, and the potholes began coming faster.

"You might want to hold on to the dash," Gabby said, swerving the car off the road to the right. On the shoulder, Gabby's car spun cyclones of dust that did not seem to dissipate.

Tires unable to latch the gravel, we spun, and the more we spun, the more Gabby pressed the accelerator until the Thunderbird felt like a power boat. We passed cars on the right, off the road. He took the Thunderbird up to seventy while the other vehicles did fifty or less. We came to a road crew with an orange barrier, two flagmen, four workers, and an asphalt layer, and we passed them to the right as well. Gabby did not slow down.

"Otay Mesa in half an hour," he yelled, like a cowboy on a galloping horse.

At certain points, the car seemed swallowed by swales in the asphalt, other times on two differing planes, a high left and a low right, or reversed, or often, a video game of potholes to dodge. Gabby broke into song, bitched about having to work when he could have retired at the age of forty, and said he longed for the mountains of his father and the pace of a small village, but I knew he was lying to please me. Gabby loved the city's electricity, long days of work, long nights of music, and sombreros on men and women to converse with, talk at, figure out, and drink.

Shortly before Tijuana but well after Tecate, Gabby swerved from the highway and took a bare earth road north toward the border. A long trail of people had lined up to cross the border, perhaps forty or fifty, most with scarves wrapped over their heads to deflect the sunshine, a few with hats, a few with no protection.

"You won't see people like this at Mexicali," he said. "People here want to be in the United States, but not the people of Mexicali. Even the people who arrive in Mexicali thinking they will escape into the U.S. end up staying and working at the factories. Let me show you the difference."

We drove and parked one block from the Tijuana River, lined with migrants and homeless and strewn with garbage.

"In Mexicali, the water runs clean. In Tijuana, dirty. In Mexicali, the factories are clean. In Tijuana, dirty. In Mexicali, the docks are cement, and in Tijuana, clay. In Mexicali, we tell the Anglos to shove it if they mistreat us. If Tijuana, they bow.

Let me show you a factory here. It will not be," he said, "the number of flies but their size that will appall you."

It was the time of the year that the fuchsia bougainvillea hung over the side of the wall and the Federales inspected trunks for kidnapped Americans, riverbanks pooled poverty, and smog and fumes made a lower layer of air that only the spire of the Catholic church pierced as if ascending for a purifying breath.

When we came to the factory, the smell of an open solder pit accosted, and on the wall of the tilt-up turned pink by the morning sun, mud swallows daubed and flickered, flies the size of a knuckle swarmed and flexed under the nests.

"When the wall gets hot, the flies electrify," Gabby said. "When the mother bird leaves, the flies raid the nest and cover the little birds like a second batch of feathers."

I drove the Thunderbird to Richard's villa, following Highway 1 to the end of Calzada Del Mar. Overlooking the Pacific Ocean, Gabby lost his restive nature. He sat on a terrace in a wicker chaise lounge without a drink and without a sound. Soon, he fell asleep, and towards evening, I covered him with a blanket. I offered him dinner, but he simply rolled his head away from me.

When the sun set, I roused and offered him food again, which he refused. He went to his room, left his clothes on, and got into bed.

The villa was more than pleasant. The adobe walls had an enticing coolness after the hot day, and I ran my hands over them every time I made a trip down a hallway, twice placing my left cheek and forehead just to dissipate the heat of a sunburn. Noiseless fans circulated in each room. The ocean air had a slight saltiness to it, as if for curing my body. I had a key to the liquor cabinet but decided to keep it locked.

Before falling asleep, I thought of the young boys who traipsed the rocks for lobsters to sell, how pleasant such a summer would have been had I lived in Rosarito as a youth.

I had to return Gabby to Mexicali and our plant by Friday

morning and then return to the U.S. that night. I shuddered to think of leaving the seaside for the desert in the Thunderbird.

Gabby woke twice during the night. The first time I found him wandering the house in his clothes, asking, "Is he there?" at every corner, behind every piece of furniture, in every room.

"Who are you looking for, Gabby," I asked.

"My father. I know he is here."

"How do you know he is here? Have you seen him?"

"No. He is a ghost."

I took Gabby by the arm and led him back to his bed.

I said, "Your father is long dead. You will only hear him in your mind, not through your ears."

"He must forgive me first before I can hear him," Gabby said. "The shaman has talked with him, has heard him. The shaman knows. The shaman."

"There is no shaman at this villa, Gabby," I whispered. "You are dreaming of your father. But it is only a dream."

Gabby grabbed both of my shoulders and shook me. "You are the one dreaming. I am awake. You are the one who thinks in a different world. I live in this one."

I got him to lie down, and he quickly fell asleep with a huge sigh.

Gabby had been with me when I received a call that I had been laid off during the business trip. I had three young children and a wife who had returned to school, debt, and no assets. I felt as though a barbell sat on my chest, and yet anxiety and panic reigned in my limbs. I was spastic in speech and motion. I felt the image of being a providing father fade from my life.

Gabby had steadied me, said those stupid cliches about hope, and said in the morning, the grass at the golf course I would run would be wet with dew even in the desert. Good times would come.

I called my wife. She said everything would be okay. But I knew it would not. I did not sleep. At dawn, I went for a run, and damn it, the grass was wet, and as I looked east over I-8, I saw moisture in the low sky making a mirror over the highway. I saw trucks hauling and cars zipping along. Life moved, and I need to move as well. I kept looking at that mirror over the road in the moisture, at hope. Al called, came over, and drove with me to San Diego, where I had to catch a flight, talking non-stop about everything but hope, job-seeking, or unemployment. He talked about cactus, tequila, wintering birds, growing apples, the taste of goat in a taco, fishing near San Felipe, women, straw hats, and how the Chinese made the mole sauce in Mexicali. I laughed, hungered.

And now it was my turn. I knew it was D.T.s withdrawal from at least alcohol, if not other drugs, but the second time he awoke screaming, shouting poetry so loudly I knew the neighbors could hear.

I let him sing his poetry until he fell, exhausted, in my arms. He was drenched in sweat, wearing only boxers, and the sheet and cover tossed to the floor.

"I've been with my ancestors," he said. "My mother lives in this poem. She is the woman loved by two men who chose only one, my father. She regretted her choice. Said he was a demon. But she was evil. She left us in spirit even though her body lived with us."

All I could do was nod.

"I left home, left my father broken, and she poisoned him. My mother killed my father, then escaped to live with the other man who loved her. When I buried him, the priest said I should never have left home."

I had heard this story before, often, and simply nodded and held him.

He recited more poetry but quietly repeated the name Flores many times, like a mantra to gain a foothold on serenity.

We rose in the early morning. Gabby woke exhausted and stayed that way. I drove the Thunderbird up Highway 1 to

Tijuana, then headed east into the sun towards Tecate, with Gabby sleeping in the back seat. The air, even in the morning, was dry, desiccating.

I kept the Thunderbird on the asphalt and drove about twenty miles per hour slower than Gabby, which meant after Tecate, we spent more time in the desert and mountains than I desired. I drove anxious about the kidnappings and finally, on the descent toward Mexicali, decided to concentrate on the fuchsia bougainvillea blooming on the walls of factories in Tijuana. It was a pleasant diversion. I noticed that Mexicali had a tremendous layer of airborne dust and smog, with a slight distorting moisture rising above the city, and as I approached saw a few mirages on the highway ahead.

Mirages. We all need mirages.

I understood now why Gabby lived in the desert, why he lived in Mexicali. When he looked off into the distance, there would be a mirage, a portal as it were, where he could imagine, finally, the voice of his father, forgiveness, even if as he approached, as I had, the mirage would disappear.

APPROPRIATE DISTANCE

Jim Daniels

My brother Tommy and I had come into some surprise money when our father died. An autoworker and child of the Great Depression, he invested in the GM savings plan and forgot about it, letting it ride till he died. He should have been doing something with our mother besides crossword puzzles and bickering.

At some point—perhaps while caring for our dying mother— he wrote in his will that Tommy and I had to take a trip outside the U.S. with the proceeds. So, my wife Caroline and I were vacationing along the Rhone River with my brother Tommy and his husband, Vic. A part of France often ignored by tourists and thus affordable to us, grandchildren of the Great Depression afraid of not speaking English and getting ripped off on our one-time splurge.

Our *chambre d'hôte* was run by Didier and Justine Crosier, who had turned their children's rooms into guest rooms after they grew up and moved to their own houses a short walk down the narrow lane next to the family vineyard. Their website claimed they spoke English, which turned out to be half-true. The four of us had taken a French class from the continuing education department at Macomb Community College, which we had disparagingly referred to as "Twelve Mile High" while growing up. Like the Crosiers, we hadn't moved far down the road, so it was an easy weekly excursion of a class: no tests, no grades. Just fun with the retired high school French teacher with the horrible accent that even we cringed at. In other words, after we'd staggered out of the train station in Lyon and into the ceremonial three air kisses, we were at the mercy of Didier and Justine.

———— ✦ ————

We were driving home from an unsuccessful mushroom-hunting trip up in the mountains. I'm sure they had a name, but the name may have been the French word for asshole. The roads angled sharply up and down hills. The flimsy guardrails looked almost theoretical. Hard to tell who was carsick and who was just sick. Didier, Caroline, and Justine rode in the car in front of us. I followed in our rental with Tommy and Vic, wishing like the Crosier children that we were at Disney instead. Even Paris Disney.

Didier's car suddenly swerved to the shoulder, spraying gravel over the edge. I hit the brakes and swerved in behind it. Had he stopped to let someone puke in the picturesque countryside?

"Wild boar!" he shouted, running toward us, Caroline in close pursuit. She'd been sitting up front with Didier. Justine had not been feeling well and was sprawled across the back seat, asleep or feigning sleep.

"You want to see wild boar, okay?" he said. He blew cigarette smoke into my face. Had Caroline let him smoke in the car? Why did they continue to smoke when their cigarette packs were stamped SMOKING KILLS in giant letters?

"Dead," he added, pointing behind us. Tommy and Vic climbed out reluctantly and in unison. This late in the day, with our meager basket of mushrooms—did anyone really need to see a dead boar?

Didier was off, heading back up the road as if it might come back to life if he didn't hurry. I headed up behind him, Caroline, and "the boys"—though they'd been together twenty-three years and officially married for five. I envied their easy way with each other, their earned grace after years of secrets and silence. I'd been with Caroline for twenty, married for nineteen.

Didier had been flirting with Caroline, lingering over those three kisses of the traditional greeting. His unshaven face scraped against hers while everybody else just got air. Justine seemed unsurprised, perhaps even amused by the way he winked and gestured at Caroline, ignoring the boys and me—maybe it was part of their schtick for their guests?

We were going through the motions of marriage, mushroom hunting, and just about everything else. Without kids to distract us, the future looked fuzzy and ill-lit. After three miscarriages, Caroline and I had stopped. We didn't want to adopt. The boys did, but the timing wasn't right—we were all too old now. They would've made great parents, Tommy and Vic—a childish joy and innocence about them that even our father failed to put a dent in. We had become a unit, the four of us. At least we should've all been in the same car.

———— ✦ ————

"A wild boar!" Tommy said, turning back to raise his eyebrows at me. "All the bores I've met, and not one of them has been wild."

I was glad to have my brother as a buffer between me and Caroline. Our shadows rose long behind us, silently overlapping as the sun angled into our faces. I'd left my sunglasses in the rental—all I could do was squint in the brightness.

After hours of trudging through woods searching for imaginary mushrooms, walking up the road's slight grade caused my hamstrings to ache. My pulse echoed in my skull. How far back up the road? Didier and Caroline had created separation on the rest of us. Didier was never subtle. Caroline liked that about him.

My job in sales forced me into casual evasion and careful deception. I had a product to sell (auto parts)—quotas to meet, numbers and people to manipulate—and I'd been pretty good at it. But there was a tipping point at Brill's Automotive, and I had tipped. I'd never become a VP or executive officer. I'd be lucky to stick it out as district manager for a dozen more years until retirement.

Caroline was a schoolteacher at the top of the pay scale, emboldened by her years of seniority that gave her a reckless charm envied and admired by colleagues and students alike.

At a bend I'd had taken too sharply while driving past, Didier stopped roadside. Caroline stood behind him, both of them, hands on hips, looking down, studying the boar as if there might be an exam on it. Or a pop quiz. Wild boars had few predators besides humans and their automobiles.

The boar was the size of a football linebacker. Bloated with death. Its coarse hairs bristled in the wind. Not much to do besides take a picture of it, so we did, both Caroline with her phone and me with mine.

"I'll send it to you, bro," I said to Tommy.

"No thanks. It's already seared into memory."

Didier nudged it with his foot. "Fell off cliff."

We all looked up at the steep rock face. I hadn't even noticed it, given our zigging and sagging.

Didier put his booted foot onto the boar's belly and pressed down, releasing gas. It made a startling grunt as a bubble of blood emerged from its nose.

"It's alive," Caroline shrieked, grabbing his shoulder. I jammed my hand inside my jacket pocket and choked the cold handle of my mushroom-cutting knife, clean, shiny, unused.

——— ✦ ———

I wanted to pack up and go home, make a gracious retreat back to the boredom of our civilized lives. I was already waving the flag of surrender— "these prices," I exclaimed to anyone who feigned listening.

Didier wielded mushroom power over us all. What was poisonous? Edible? His tenderness with Caroline, his gruffness with me. I swore I'd found a couple that were edible, but each time, Didier laughed, shook his head, and turned away.

The brightest mushrooms, the surreal red ones, were apparently the most poisonous. If you're poisonous, shouldn't you be harder to notice? You weren't even supposed to touch them, but I felt a certain allure as I hovered over one large, beautiful one. I half understood Caroline's attraction to Didier.

———— ✦ ————

"There are many kinds of betrayal," Tommy said. "And we've lived long enough to see them all…" He kept nodding into the silence that followed.

I had hesitated to tell them, but of course I did. They had this thing with Caroline—a gossipy, campy level of overly caffeinated exchanges that had become a tired routine over the years, but it seemed like no one could stop it.

"I can't believe it myself," I said, though of course I did. Caroline could treat Tommy and Vic like ornamental pet poodles. In fact, she petted them and sometimes talked baby talk to them. All nudge nudge, wink wink. A stale situation comedy on automatic pilot, and it was time for the shark to jump, and I was poking that shark with a cattle prod.

———— ✦ ————

You can hunt mushrooms without stealth—you can't startle a mushroom into fleeing. The knives cut them off at the stem. If you just yanked them, you'd destroy the spores, and they wouldn't regenerate. I couldn't even find any, though, much less damage them. I, who had failed to regenerate.

Didier wore an unlikely jeweled machete on a belt around his waist, which did not look as ridiculous as it sounds. Didier could pull it off with his barrel-bellied swagger. He was born to wear that machete. Caroline had taken numerous photos of him posing with it.

———— ✦ ————

"Go over here," Didier said to Caroline. "Spread out." He pointed with his machete. It makes me laugh, that word: machete. It hurts too, but I invest a lot in that word now, telling the story, the long version of the longer version of the short version of what led us back to Detroit early. On the surface, I was taking a stand to support my brother. Who could argue with that? I mean, besides my brother.

"Let's leave them over there, hunting fairies," Didier snorted.

Behind a row of pines, walking carefully on sharp, brown needles, I couldn't see Caroline's reaction. It would have been easy to pretend I didn't hear, and that was my habit. I wasn't going to confront Didier. He'd treated the boys well enough, and you could take his remark with a certain ambiguity, given the language challenges.

But then Caroline's open-mouthed laugh pierced like one of those dry needles. It needed no translation. I knew that laugh well enough to picture it. "Fairies hunting for fairies," she said. It seemed so overtly cruel that I stopped, stunned with surprise. Was she riffing off Didier's bluntness?

"Eddie's the worst of them," she added. Eddie, that's me. I coughed loudly, then kicked a rock. I admit, it was childish, lame—I was out of my element. Unsure what my element was anymore.

Our father's generosity was a burden, and Caroline and I had enough burdens. I was my father's son—Caroline and I stopped taking vacations after my mother became too ill to sit in a beach chair for a week. She couldn't read anymore, due to partial blindness. She said the sound of the ocean made her dizzy, so far from suburban Detroit, where we all still lived. Now that all of our parents were dead, we had no excuse for not taking vacations, but we seemed to have forgotten how.

———— ✦ ————

I didn't quite believe in wild boars either—at least, not the wild marauding hordes of them that Didier claimed surrounded us. We went for long walks on the well-marked French hiking trails through the woods and saw a few bored hunters smoking cigarettes, shotguns casually arranged in their arms while their agitated hounds chased phantom smells through the woods.

Tommy and I had both been given shotguns for our fourteenth birthday by our grandfather, along with enrollment in a gun safety class. I'd actually gone hunting a few times—it was clear to Tommy, and to me, pretty early on that he was gay, but for the rest of the family, it was tickets to football games and hunting classes. Though I resented carrying the manly burden, I was certainly no poster child for a sensitive soul who supported gay rights. But he was my brother, and when he found Vic, and they seemed so happy together, I got it—maybe I got it too much, comparing the energy and care they still gave to their relationship to what Caroline and I had settled into.

———— ✦ ————

I felt a surge of something as we walked back to the car—adrenaline? Shame? It was almost as if seeing the boar, the boar blood, the husky putrid exhale of gas, had made my life tangible. Rustling through the scrubby brush of that rocky countryside, watching my wife flirt with Didier challenged my—yeah, okay, my manhood. We had stayed too long. Perhaps we should have split it into two trips. Maybe we should have warmed up with Canada first. We'd been across the border to gamble at the casino but had never ventured beyond Windsor, an industrial town not dissimilar to Detroit.

———— ✦ ————

"Why'd you call me a fairy to Didier?" I hissed as soon as we were alone together at the rear of the roadside parade back to the cars. I pulled on her arm to slow her down. Tommy pulled Vic forward. Didier led the charge, his machete clanking against his side. He'd protect us in order to make fools of us. Maybe that's why Justine stayed in the car—she didn't want to see it. Maybe she was imagining it now with her eyes closed in the backseat of the car, and the door swung open.

"It was just a play on words. Loosen up, will you?" She pulled away. "You're wasting your father's money."

"You were complicit," I said, poking a finger at her, grinding my feet to a stop in the roadside gravel.

She laughed, a mocking sneer. "Complicit!" she shouted.

"You're too much." She paused.

"Tommy and Vic. I don't care about me," I said, though of course I did.

"He didn't mean anything. He doesn't know—maybe calling them fairies is perfectly okay in French."

"Yeah, let's look that up when we get home," I said.

A slow car chugged past, followed by a half-dozen serious tailgaters waiting for a clear stretch to pass, though that mountain road offered few opportunities.

"We'd better get moving," she said.

"I told Tommy," I said. "My *fairy* brother."

For some reason, Didier had turned around at the car and was headed back toward us. "Let's ask Didier if it's perfectly okay," I said. My hands trembled slightly.

"Now you're a tattletale! As if you never made fun of them," she said and began rushing forward again. For a moment, it looked like she was going to take his arm. When I returned to the car, Tommy and Vic sat hunched together, waiting for me in late afternoon shadow, the sun sinking behind the cliff face. Darkness was imminent.

For years, my biggest secret was that I'd shot my own brother—buckshot, in the ass, no harm done—by accident. Tommy knew what trouble I'd be in if our father found out. My biggest secret, a harmless one, had now turned into a family joke, not like the trajectory of his secret, which oozed out in slow motion and got replayed over and over again.

I picked out a couple pieces of shot with the needle-nose pliers on my Leatherman right in the woods and bandaged it up when we got home.

———— ✦ ————

Justine sat up in the other car and rubbed her eyes. Were we a mirage? Had it all been just a dream? We'd paid in cash, in advance, as requested. Justine squinted and gave me a mysterious smile as if I was the one wearing the machete.

I stood roadside in the middle of that beautiful nowhere. Rushing wind surged past, rustling the roadside trees. I kept turning around, thinking a car was coming, but no car was coming. I looked at our meager basket of dirty mushrooms in the backseat next to Justine, which was intended to be a feature of our farewell meal. Someone had been over the same stretch of woods ahead of us and had gotten all the big mushrooms. Maybe a wild boar—they eat anything, apparently.

I put my hand on Didier's shoulder. Knowing we were leaving soon, he allowed his smile to turn into a slight grimace outside the open car door.

"I shot my brother once," I said. "I don't know how that translates, but I just wanted you to know." I should have rented a translator for my own idiocy.

Tommy poked his head out of the rental. "It's true," he said, leaning out. "But I forgave him!"

Didier unstrapped his machete without a word, and then we were off again, the road, all downhill. I flicked on my brights and followed them at an unsafe distance.

———— ✦ ————

Back in our room across the hall from Tommy and Vic's room, Caroline and I lay in bed together. She had apologized to them. I had apologized to them for trying to turn them against Caroline. I apologized to her for telling them. She apologized to me for embarrassing me. I apologized to my dead father for squandering his money and for finding no mushrooms. Apologies all the way around. Then we held each other in the eerie silence of that beautiful countryside. I will spare you those apologies, with all their sincere imperfections. I've learned that many famous painters came to the south of France for the quality of light, but it was the quality of the silence I appreciated then, the dark silence that pressed us together despite our meager selves.

———— ✦ ————

The easiest thing in the world would have been to pack up and go home—retreat— a day early, and that's what we did in the morning. I apologized to Didier as we departed. We gave each other three kisses. Despite knowing the appropriate distance, I leaned into the scratch of his unshaven face.

A CONVERSATION WITH JIM DANIELS

Lowestoft Chronicle Interview by Nicholas Litchfield
(February 2024)

Jim Daniels
(Photograph courtesy of Jim Daniels)

Author, editor, and scriptwriter Jim Daniels, a man with forty-two books and four independent films to his name, has had a long and distinguished literary career. His many awards include a Devine Fellowship in poetry, selected by Pulitzer Prize winner Galway Kinnell; the Wisconsin/ Brittingham Prize for Poetry, judged by Pulitzer Prize winner C. K. Williams; two fellowships from the National Endowment for the Arts, and two from the Pennsylvania Council on the Arts. His poems— some anthologized in the Pushcart Prize and Best American Poetry, some recited on *A Prairie Home Companion* and NPR's *All Things Considered*—have been featured on Garrison Keillor's *The Writer's Almanac*, in Billy Collins' *Poetry 180* anthologies, and Ted Kooser's national newspaper column "American Life in Poetry." One of his poems was even reproduced on the roof of a race car.

In this exclusive interview with *Lowestoft Chronicle*, Daniels discusses his most recent fiction collection, his new chapbook, and the remarkable attention his first full-length poetry collection drew.

Lowestoft Chronicle (LC): *The Luck of the Fall,* published by Michigan State University Press last year, is a moving collection where, to put it broadly, the past plays a principal role in characters' thoughts, outlooks, and impulses. The voices are varied, and the tone and style of the writing differ throughout. You also cover all sorts of heavy subjects, including addiction and recovery, grief, and mental illness. How did this collection take shape? What's the unifying theme? And did you write these thirteen stories with the intention of publishing them together in one volume?

Jim Daniels (JD): I've written many stories on similar themes from one book to the next. Many of them are set in the Detroit area where I grew up and where I still have a lot of family and friends. Detroit has had its share of hard times over the years, and some of those affect the lives of the characters in these stories. While I didn't have that kind of intentionality in terms of the collection, I certainly was aware of links between individual stories. Usually, when I accumulate what I think is a decent number of finished stories, I get a feeling that maybe it's time for another book and pull out everything since the last book and see what I have. All the potential stories don't make it into the book because they don't end up fitting the shape that begins to form once I spread out the stories and see how they interact with each other as I play around with the order. In other words, hunch has a lot to do with it. For me at least, the title story for this book seemed to capture the tone of a number of the stories—that failure can bring with it something we might define as luck, or at least some kind of consolation.

It's funny that I do a lot of traveling now that I'm semi-retired from teaching, but I continue to write a lot about where I grew up. For me, I think the sense of place, the setting, tends to be pretty important. I like to write about traveling when I'm in a place long enough to get a sense of life beneath the surface in whatever community I happen to be in.

LC: The titular story, also the opener, is an observance of youth and innocence and a commiseration on the loss of innocence. It's a wonderfully circular story with a perfect first sentence. First of all, how important are first sentences? Was the opening the starting point for the story, or were the first lines the last thing you wrote to tie in the ending and give lyrical balance to the narrative? The story appears in the *North American Review* summer 2023 volume. Did you write it with NAR in mind?

JD: Thanks. Oh, yes, the first sentences are very important for me. As important as the title, often. Particularly coming from my background as a poet, I always try to create an immediacy with the opening, to get into it as quickly as possible without too much backstory, making the story feel top-heavy.

You're certainly right in noticing that the past plays a big role in many of the stories. I feel like "The Heart-Attack Bear" is dominated by the past, for the main character, at least, so my challenge there was to show a character living in the past while also showing how it affects his present life to achieve a balance, to try to avoid the story itself being nostalgic for the past when the main character himself is nostalgic.

While I didn't write "The Luck of the Fall" with the *North American Review* in mind, I have been fortunate enough to find them receptive to both my stories and poems over the years. I really enjoy reading the magazine, and the title story seemed like a good fit. It was the first place I submitted it, so I was very happy they took it. One of the things that has sustained me over the years is the support for certain journals that have stayed with me over the decades.

LC: You gave an interview for *Superstition Review* many years ago (I think it may have been in 2008), and one of the questions concerned how fatherhood affects your writing. That question was related to a poetry collection, but I think the essence of it is pertinent to this collection, too. A story like "The Spirit Award," where a boy yearns for love and validation from his somewhat aloof and detached father, provokes scrutiny of one's own parenting skills. What was the motivation behind this story? How challenging is it to adopt the perspective of an adolescent and seem authentic?

JD: I think that story came from a number of places. First, as a parent, I witnessed the political aspect of youth sports, the fathers in particular taking it way too seriously. But part of it involves my relationship with my own father. He was working a lot of overtime when I was young and playing sports, and he missed most of my games—in fact, whole seasons, and that opportunity created some emotional distance between us. He himself was a star athlete in high school, and I think it saddens us both a little that we missed a potential connection back when I was a kid. I have to admit, I wasn't much of an athlete, like the main character in the story. In my last season of high school basketball, I scored one point the entire year. Enough said.

LC: Regarding your short fiction, you've filled seven volumes (including one formed from flash fiction pieces), and two-time Oscar-nominated director/screenwriter John Sayles extolled praise on characters in *Trigger Man*, one of those collections. You've even published four screenplays, each of which have been independent films. Have you written any novels, and are there other mediums you'd like to explore (perhaps stage plays or radio dramas)?

JD: I really started out as a poet, and I continue to write a lot of poetry, so, for me, a short story can seem long. I've written some pretty long stories, but nothing approaching a novel—though I read novels all the time. I have been writing more essays lately, and will have a collection of those, *An Ignorance of Trees*, forthcoming in 2025 from Cornerstone Press. I did write a couple of one-act plays that got produced here and there by small theater companies. I also really enjoyed the process of collaboration on the low-budget films, and I've worked with a photographer, Charlee Brodsky, on two books that combine her photos and my poems, so I would like to find more opportunities to work with artists in other fields. John Sayles is one of my heroes—both through his fiction and his films, he has maintained his individuality and independence as an artist and has never been afraid to try new things.

LC: When it comes to poems, my assumption has always been that, by and large, chapbooks and volumes of poetry tend to go unnoticed by leading publications. But this doesn't seem to be the case with your work. Careful appraisals of your verse feature in venues like the *Village Voice*, the *Wall Street Journal*, and multiple times in the *New York Times Book Review*. Were you surprised by the attention and accolades your first full-length collection, *Places/Everyone*, received? What impact did winning the inaugural Brittingham Prize in Poetry have on your writing?

JD: You are certainly correct in that assumption. This is particularly true of chapbooks, but I've always liked the intensity and thematic unity you can create in the shorter form, and I also like how attractive many chapbooks are—I've had a few gorgeous letterpress collections over the years. I was very lucky that *Places/Everyone* got quite a bit of attention and helped launch my career. I was definitely surprised! I was also lucky that the Brittingham Prize has continued over the years and gained in stature, with many notable poets being selected. It'll be going on forty years next year. At this point in my writing life, I am happy to continue to find an audience, however small, for my writing.

LC: "Jim Daniels is a kind of Bruce Springsteen of the poetry world. Or, in keeping with his Michigan roots, perhaps a Bob

Seger," wrote Roger Gilles of the daily newspaper *The Grand Rapids Press*. "The result is every bit as powerful as anything Springsteen or Seger have produced." It's always great to receive positive endorsements, but have you ever felt pressure when putting together a collection, such as a fear of not living up to expectations?

JD: Well, that's pretty hyperbolic, but I'll take the praise. One of my recent books was *RESPECT: The Poetry of Detroit Music,* an anthology of poetry and lyrics about the city. Music has been one of the great exports from Detroit, along with, of course, cars, so Springsteen and Seger, particularly in terms of their songs that capture working-class life, have been an influence on me.

I'm a fairly obsessive writer, so I'm always working on something, so I produce a lot. I think, however, particularly with poetry, my expectations for recognition tend to be pretty low.

LC: Your newest collection, *Comment Card,* was published by Carnegie Mellon University Press a few days ago. It's your thirty-second collection. How does this chapbook differ from prior work, and what can your readers expect?

JD: Particularly for a chapbook, this has less of a tight focus. I think this is my first collection that does not have the word "Detroit" in it, and I think that's a significant departure readers might notice. Family continues to play a significant role in this collection, though the perspective comes from an older person with grown children of his own.

I don't think any writer wants to get pigeonholed, and I'm no exception. I want to continue to grow and try new things—to surprise myself and, hopefully, my readers as well.

THE MÉRIDA EXPRESS

Lorraine Caputo

I. 19 December 1997 / 6:45 a.m. / Córdoba, Veracruz

Day is just breaking. The air is cool and damp.

The Mexico City train has finally arrived…late. We, its newest passengers, stumble across the tracks to where these two lone cars await their locomotive.

As I settle in for this ride—one of Mexico's most infamous hell rides, ratty and eternally late—my mind creates a variation on a late-1960s song: *Don't you know we're riding on the Mérida Express… They're taking me to Mérida… All aboard the train… All abroad the train…*

II.

I drift out of memories of the dream I had before awakening at four to catch this train.

We are passing by miles and miles of tasseling sugarcane. The morning mist swirls over blades of cane and around flowering mango trees, around banana trees, around orange trees heavy with fruit.

A man sings a ditty, holding up boxes of vitamins: "Oh, you can have a woman so beautiful. Oh, but on the inside, she could be oh, so sick. And with these vitamins… Only ten *pesitos*…."

Teenage girls giggle at his comments. Men snigger and sneer.

But as the vendor walks the length of the car, people pull the ten-peso note for those red and black magic pills from out of their pockets. The face of Emiliano Zapata watches as his banknote is passed from hand to hand.

We now pass through a narrow valley. Sugarcane stretches out to those green mountains swathed in misty clouds. Those mountains look like mango trees. Oh, and the mango trees—like clouds.... There are so many villages all along, so many houses made of scrap wood boards, of scrap tin.

III. 10:10 a.m. / Tierra Blanca, Veracruz

The car in front of us is unhooked and pulled away by the locomotive. The woman next to me says assuredly, a third one will be added.

Amid the flow of more passengers into the car, vendors pour onboard with buckets of drinks, plates of food. They can barely push by the people without seats.

I sip atole to take off the chill. Its warmth brings back memories of Gran Salinas ruins in New Mexico, of Fito sneaking off somewhere to make a fire, and coming back with a steamy pot. All the way back to Albuquerque, we four—his brother in the front seat, me and a friend in the back—drink atole from the blue corn Fito grew.

The sun brightens my window as it weakly tears at the clouds. Along the ground, aside from our car, dogs sniff for chicken bones tossed out windows. A boy rides a donkey down the street.

Across the aisle, from the overhead rack, a father strings a hammock for his son. The young one suckles his mother's breast.

We begin traveling again, just one car. A huge troupe of buzzards flies up off the tracks we approach.

Our train passes truck upon truck, railcars upon railcars overflowing with cut sugarcane. A man sits in his yard husking corn. Those mountains are now farther off.

You know what kind of clouds mango trees remind me of? The kind that brings summer storms—flat on the bottom and towering, billowing, into the heavens.

IV. 1:15 p.m. / Approaching La Palma

We're traveling through a vast patchwork. Various shades of green, various textures drape across the landscape. Fields of pineapples, fallow fields, pastures.

At the side of the tracks, *zopilotes* cast their shadows over a dead cow.

We clack past small towns of cabañas with palm-thatch roofs and cane-slat walls stuccoed over and rarely painted.

V. 3:15 p.m. / Los Tigres

We are still 45 kilometers from Medias Aguas. We will probably be there in over an hour. The train stopped briefly at this station in the middle of these flatlands.

Two women came aboard with large baskets. They call out, "Chicken, tacos, tortillas, rice, *chile relleno, milanesa*." The train's porter follows right behind, selling soft drinks and beer.

VI. 5:37 p.m. / Stopped south of Medias Aguas, in the middle of nowhere

I took a break from sitting for a while and let a mother with her two children sit.

Aboard is a young man, his hair greying already. He wears four layers of filthy shirts beneath a holey sweater. His pants are several sizes too big and held up with a rope. The tennis shoes are mismatched, one held together with a string tied around the sole. I hand him a few tacos.

It's going to be a long night—no lights in this car, that screeching kid, and the humidity. I pop an aspirin.

Dusk has fallen, and now it's too dark to write. People rush to move their belonging down from the racks to the floor in front of their seats.

The trees are getting restless. I wonder if a storm is a-coming.

It's going to be a long, long night.

VII. 8 p.m. / Just past Chinameca, Veracruz

I am awakened by a conversation between a woman from Chiapas sitting next to me and a man in the aisle. I am held by the edge in her voice and his replies.

"It's a disgrace how they treat us passengers," she says.

"Indeed, it is," he replies.

"Not giving us another car, making us squeeze into this one. Especially when there are so many people traveling now with the holidays."

"Yes," the *señor* says.

"But there aren't any extra cars. They're using them all to transport soldiers to the south." Since the Zapatista uprising in her home state, many troops have been mobilized in that region.

"No, you don't have that right," the man states firmly. "It's to transport soldiers and *federales* to the north, to Chihuahua, to fight against the narcotraffickers."

"No, to move soldiers to the *south*."

"No. It isn't as simple as that. It's much more complex." He spits on the ground, leaving a mark on his pant leg.

VIII. 20 December / 7:30 a.m. / Macuspana, Tabasco

This is my second dawn upon this train that once again is nothing more than the lightening of a clouded sky and still the steady light rain. The morning mists swirl around the jungle-covered mountains. The sun is beginning to break through the clouds. Canes and vines brush against our train.

We pass a village. Most of the houses are built of rough board and roofed with tin. Turkeys waddle in the yards. One fans his ragged tail wide.

IX. 11:43 a.m. / Tenosique, Tabasco

We have been stopped here now for 20 minutes. A whole chorus of women's voices—from young girls to *abuelitas* (grandmothers)—chants their noonday offerings.

Hay empanadas

Hay tacos de pollo

Hay empanadas
Hay arroz con leche
Hay tacos de pollo
Hay empanadas
Hay empanadas

I buy three chicken tacos and a cup of rice and milk.

A musical family board. Father plays guitar and sings, a son plays *güiro* and takes tips. Someone plays an electric keyboard, drowning out the rest of them.

It is now 12:13 p.m., and a train is blowing its horn. Is it this one? As soon as I write the words, our train jerks forward, and on we go...

X. 3:33 p.m. / Don Samuel, Campeche

I chuckle as we pass the primary school named after Emiliano Zapata. (Again, he appears during this train journey. He's staring at me...)

XI. 5:38 p.m. / Wherever

My second dusk upon this train is falling.

Some say we will be in Mérida at about 2 a.m., others say no, 9 or 10 a.m. We'll see... we'll see...

We had been passing through the heavily wooded, rolling flatlands of Campeche State. Sometimes we dip into a cut-through in these low hills.

And now this, my second night upon this train, is beginning.

And I settle into a meditation on the purpose of my life. And I scold myself for my failings, my laziness.

XII. 7:40 p.m. / Campeche City

We've just pulled into here. According to the train schedule, it's four more hours to Mérida. But if this trip so far is any indication...

A group of soldiers come aboard and begin checking baggage. Their lights flash across the ceiling. I look out the window. More soldiers, rifles slung over their shoulders, walk the platform.

I quietly ask another passenger, "Why are there so many of them?"

In the darkness comes an answer. "They're looking for drugs and other contraband. If you look suspicious, they'll haul you and your belongings off."

The vendors rush on with heavy baskets and jugs.

> *Hay pollo*
> *Hay tamalitos*
> > *Hay jugo*
> > *refrescos*
> > *agua purificada*
> *Hay pollo*
> *Hay tamalitos*
> > *Hay Nescafé*
> > *Hay arroz con leche*

As the soldiers leave, people stare after them.

With a stomach full of tamales and pineapple juice, I snuggle down for a nap. We leave Campeche at 8:15, finally with a second car.

XIII. 21 December / 3:35 a.m. / Mérida, Yucatán

I found an open eatery just around the corner from the station. A cup of coffee warms my hand.

The train for Izamal, my next destination, leaves at 6 a.m.

We arrived here at 3:05 a.m.—44 hours later—and over 17 hours late.

LIGHT IN MEXICO

George Moore

in memoriam Tony Ostroff

The light you wrote of at war's edge
that light fused to rose adobe

not of the jungles where so many bled
not of the barricades that stood against

whatever would disturb that light
whatever would yank us out of our desks

that glow of sunset dust on an old street
where two children ran and a tourist woman

tries to capture in her paints their fleeing
while the light was just right just rose

and it was not a place for death but light
and yet both were passing

We can almost return to it
but you are dead and the slender volume

now snug between a thousand friends
cries out on this northern shelf

occupies more than the lines say
a space in time that recuperates

the value of the time itself
as if cupped in these hands

But it is the silence that I remember
the sudden silence when gunfire ceases

the others their terror in the jungles
the dusty streets across which I ran

before the paint dries and we
are pressed between the pages

THE FIRES

George Moore

The wind some wanted to blame
the wind as if it had come up fast

out of revenge for all the building
onto the open prairie open to flame

but I think of the ticky-tacky song
of houses Pete Seeger sings

and how childhood catches fire then
how all of the rooms are consumed

and nothing left but a one-eyed bear
sleeping or leaning dead in a corner

where no one is left to claim her
but the fire the quick and friendly fire

For the neighbors the tragedy
is insurance not the flames eating

the white curtains or the new lawnmower
blowing up in the well swept garage

but how the insurance becomes
a maze with the Minotaur waiting

at the center that is no center
and the ruins three thousand years old

and no one to blame that is it
really the dead-end of who to blame

no one but the furies and Boreas
no one who signed anything

And for the town it is a tragedy
of where the homeless dogs can sleep

where the deer have fled what
possible motive for this madness

as if someone were in charge
and the elements their tools

But fire consumes itself is its own end
we live with it in our hearts

we breath it at each other the fire
of the bombed-out buildings

the fires of Dresden and Ukraine
the fire we keep in its hidden jar

the genii we believe will save us
even as we are consumed

TWO DAYS OUT FROM SAN JUAN

Mark Jacobs

Two days out from San Juan, on the Pinnacle's fifth deck, Wilson was pouring wine for the Profesora. His luck was changing; his ruination would come to pass.

"You are a man, Wilson," the Profesora said.

"More Chardonnay, *señora*?"

She looked like the blonde mother-in-law in a *telenovela*. She put her hand flat over the glass to indicate she'd had enough and began again. "You are a man, Wilson Peñaranda, of music and muscle."

Three tables down, serving drinks to a rowdy crowd of sunburned cruisers, the Turk stole a glance and caught the effect of the Profesora's words on Wilson. Nazim was a sour little man with whom, this trip, Wilson shared a cabin. He had to put up with the Turk's depression, which he put on in the morning like socks. Things had been worse lately since Wilson had offended his roommate. He could not recall what he had said, he'd been so full of Red Stripe. All he remembered was an out-of-the-way Jamaican bar that smelled of diesel and fish and the Turk's hurt expression.

"I'm not flattering you," the Profesora told him, "I'm stating a fact. Remind me, please, where we dock in the morning."

"Raimundo will inform you of tomorrow's schedule, *señora*. That duty falls to the waiter."

"As it falls to his assistant to keep the dinner guests happy."

He admired the quick comeback.

There was confusion in the galley that night, which was staffed by Filipinos and Caribbean people, with an Indian overlord who knew how to make their lives miserable. The confusion had a ricochet effect on the wait staff. The upshot was that Wilson's head did not hit the pillow until midnight, and he had to be on his feet again by five. He was working the early breakfast shift. He had little patience for the Turk.

"A rich woman with yellow hair and a diamond on her finger large enough to feed three villages. Not a woman for you, Wilson. Her ancestors scourged the backs of men like you."

Wilson apologized again for having wounded the man. "If you tell me what it was I said back in Jamaica, I will say I am sorry and mean it."

But Nazim would not give up his grudge. As long as Wilson did not remember the insult, it remained the worst thing one human being had ever said to another.

As Nazim went on talking, an intense blue yearning settled on Wilson. He was home. Above the floodline, under palms flapping noisily in a hot wind, a wooden house painted red. A tin roof. In the bed, a fine woman lay on her side, nursing his son. There was a rocking chair alongside the bed. Wilson sat there rocking in the pride of fatherhood.

Discouragement would follow his yearning for home. It always did. As the immense engines of the Pinnacle of the Seas powered the cruise ship toward St. Vitus in the British Virgin Islands, sleep was the only way out.

———— ✦ ————

At breakfast, an accident. Raimundo cut his finger while slicing bread. The cut went deep, and Wilson took his place just as the Profesora was choosing her table. She was dressed to tour the island in a white blouse, blue shorts, sandals with straps. She looked expensive. He watched her fingers tear apart a croissant and asked her what she taught.

"Political science. I focus on Latin America. The Southern Cone."

That explained her Spanish.

She switched suddenly to English. "Are you going ashore, Wilson?"

"I have a couple of hours free."

"Then let me buy you a cold drink."

"They don't like us to socialize with the guests."

She nodded as if that made sense but said, "You'll find me."

He did, of course. St. Vitus was small, poor, beautiful. Little of the island's British past was visible except for the policemen's uniforms, crisp in the killer heat. Four blocks up from the beach, the touristic façade was gone, and in a poor man's bar where her white skin made her stand out, the Profesora sat waiting for him.

"Don't worry," she said, inviting him to sit across from her at a rickety plastic table. "If anybody says something, I forced you. I made you sit with me. Shall we try the rum?"

Rum was a bad idea. It made Wilson aware of details: her scent, the pull of her breasts beneath the fabric of her blouse, a fixation in her green eyes.

"I scare you," she said.

"I'm not scared."

"For the record, I'm not interested in a cross-cultural adventure. And I'm not lonely."

"That's good."

"I love my job. Richard—that's my husband—owns three automobile dealerships in Pittsburgh. We think the world of each other."

"I also love my wife. I love my son."

"What are their names?"

He told her.

"You are a beautiful man. Tell me something about yourself."

"From the house of my parents, I could throw a stone into the sea."

"The Dominican Republic, right?"

He nodded, nostalgic, saying the name of his home. "Santa Barbara de Samaná. Cruise ships stop there. I used to go down to the pier and watch the people get off."

"So it was your fate to sail on the Pinnacle."

The word 'fate' was ominous in her mouth. He lied, telling her he was due back on the ship in twenty minutes.

"Tomorrow is St. Kitts," she said. "Don't tell me you will have no free time."

He thanked her for the drink and left the bar. Out on the street, he wandered, enjoying the feel of solid earth under his feet, until he bumped into the Turk, who was ogling a group of local women.

"Hello, shipmate. Did you enjoy your drink with the diamond lady?"

"What drink?"

"A simple question."

His smugness angered Wilson. Overreacting, he shoved Nazim. Not hard, but the Turk stumbled backward and fell in the street next to a skinny yellow cur that yelped.

He smiled, getting to his feet.

"We will see, my handsome friend. We will see what happens now."

Wilson regretted making an enemy out of his berthmate, but he still seethed.

"What will we see, Nazim??"

"Strong or smart." Nazim wiped his mouth with the back of his hand. "Which wins?"

That evening in the dining room Wilson took pains to keep his distance from Nancy. That was what she had requested he call her. She was seated with a party of Japanese cruisers. As Wilson delivered bread to their table, she said in calm Spanish, "I hope I didn't get you in any trouble."

He smiled. "No problem, *señora*."

Later, lying on his bunk, before he switched off his reading lamp Nazim seemed contrite. "It was a misunderstanding. You will forgive me."

"A misunderstanding," Wilson agreed. "And you will forgive whatever it was I said to you in Jamaica."

"Of course."

He didn't mean it, but Wilson let it go. He was suffering through one of his periodic bouts of jealousy. Bezi. He was away from home so often, she must be tempted by another man. Right now, some son of a bitch from Samaná was turning her head with sexy talk and shrimp in garlic sauce.

A little later, the Turk's snoring brought Wilson back to where he was. Where he had to stay in order to provide for his family. He slept.

———— ◆ ————

St. Kitts was a lot like St. Vitus, an independent country if you could call reliance on the kindness of cruise-ship strangers independence. There was a belief that the British had interrupted Paradise when they colonized the place. Wilson believed that was nonsense. Before the British, there had been slow turtles, dim fish, trees that grew until they fell over in the forest. At any rate, he had explored the island half a dozen times on previous trips and thought about staying on board to catch up on his sleep. But when Raimundo told him he was free for three hours, he left the ship to meet his destiny head-on.

On the pier, just past customs, scrawny St. Kitts men dressed like Rastafarians held up little monkeys as the tourists disembarked. To Wilson, it seemed shameful for all concerned, but some of the cruisers were paying five dollars to have their picture taken with the phony Rastas and their tame monkeys. He went past them, not looking for Nancy.

There came a moment. A pastel blouse. A voice that came out rich in English. An absence of diamond on her slim finger. Up from the beach, a grove of squatty palms. Under the palms, a mature woman unbuttoned her blouse. Shed her skirt. Wilson had never seen a woman so completely at her naked ease.

"I want to pay tribute," she said, sitting cross-legged on a blue towel she had spread on the sand.

Wilson said nothing. A slat of shade from the palm fronds

protected her bare breasts. She was aggravated by his failure to speak.

"Say my name."

"Nancy."

"You are perfect, Wilson. What God was thinking about when he came up with the idea for Man."

The sex was a frenzy. She wanted him to talk. She didn't mind what he said; it was the coffee in his voice, the thunderstorm in a high sky, hot oil in a pan she wanted. Once or twice she whimpered, but it was not distress. It was not ecstasy, either. It was freefall.

All the time he was inside her, he was aware of a sadness, like a beggar tugging at his sleeve. Not until he and Nancy had dressed and parted, sneaking out of their hiding place separately, did he recognize his sadness as homesickness. Walking toward the pier, he felt complicated. Relief mingled with a sense of accomplishment. The vision of Nancy's comfortable body would sustain him through long days. But the sadness kept tugging at him. His wife was eating *tostones* with a strange man who was thinking nasty as he poured her a drink.

Pierside, he knew. Instantly. Grooms was standing in a square of shade on the wrong side of the customs turnstile, holding a suitcase. Grooms was Trinidadian, a burly Black man of fifty who looked military in his white uniform. He ran the wait staff like an army.

"Peñaranda."

Wilson joined him in the shade alongside a government building of some sort, newly whitewashed to maintain the colonial look.

"You're finished."

"I don't follow you."

"Yes, you do. You broke the cardinal rule."

It must have been Nazim. He had followed Wilson to the palm grove and seen the Profesora go in.

"The goddamned Turk," Wilson said.

Grooms smiled thin. He relaxed his shoulders and fanned his face with his uniform hat. "This is Nazim's last contract with us. When we hit San Juan, he's out."

"I can explain."

"No, you can't."

He handed Wilson an envelope. "This is what we owe you, plus enough to fly you back home." He gave him his suitcase, which was square and old-fashioned, held shut with a bungee cord. It had belonged, years back, to Bezi's father.

Wilson's vision blurred as his eyes teared. He had promised Bezi a washing machine. Hadn't Grooms ever screwed up?

"My wife's name is Bezi."

Grooms nodded sympathetically. "Go home and kiss her. Then find yourself another job."

Wilson was so wrapped up in the misery of the moment he did not notice Nancy until she was standing there with them in the shaded oasis.

"Is there a problem?"

"No problem, Madam," Grooms reassured her.

If Grooms had an opinion about a passenger having sex in the sand with an assistant waiter, she would never know it. Wilson was aware of the smell of her. In one hand, he held the envelope Grooms had given him; in the other hand, his suitcase. He did not trust himself to speak, so he turned away.

"No," said Nancy with conviction. "This is not happening."

"You'll want to board, Madam," Grooms told her. "We'll be departing momentarily."

"But it's not his fault. The whole thing was my fault."

That was decent of her, trying to save him, although her attempt to fix things only demonstrated her ignorance of the world's workings. She ran after him and yanked his arm, breathing hard.

"Wilson, I'm sorry. I am so very sorry."

He wanted her to suffer, not for having made love with him but for being so intelligent and knowing so little. He moved away.

"Stop," she said.

He stopped.

"What will you do?"

He shrugged.

She was going through her purse, coming up with money. She folded the bills into a wad. He made a fist into which it would not enter. It wasn't pride that prevented him from taking money he needed. It was a sense of duty. He owed himself respect for the fate that had befallen him. Had he not sought it out?

"Please," she pleaded. "I feel so terrible, Wilson. I'll feel worse if you don't take it."

A smaller man would point out that how she felt was beside the point.

"You had better board," he told her.

There was no satisfaction in letting the air out of her. He was distant from the pier when the Pinnacle sailed.

Later, he wandered back to the pier, looking for a travel office to book a flight home. He was not ready to face Bezi, to kiss the top of William's head, smell the clean smell of shampoo and little boy. Later, he could not remember how he fell into a conversation with Trevor.

"They threw you off the big white ship, didn't they? That's an evil thing to do to a man."

"I quit."

"Sure, sure. Without a doubt."

Trevor had a monkey named Lulu, a Rasta get-up heavy on purple, braids in his beard, and a broad face that revealed his emotions before he himself knew what he was feeling.

"Maybe I get myself a monkey," Wilson said, seeking to injure himself. "Maybe I buy a suit of pretend Jamaica clothes and go around saying don't worry, be happy, 'mon."

"You need food."

He led Wilson to his mother's house, where she stuffed him full of rice and fried fish, and salty shallots. She was a large woman who demanded no explanations. The two men ate like long friends who did not require words with their meal.

Wilson had a sense of time passing. He needed distraction and the chance to make another mistake. Which he did. It took a while, but when he lay down to sleep on a pallet in a back room at Trevor's mother's house, he had gambled away the money in the envelope Grooms had given him. He lost most of it to a friend of Trevor's with a bent back and a pirate's eyepatch who spoke in Rasta parables and threw the dice with flair. Once or twice, Trevor had tried to put the brakes on Wilson.

"Live with what you don't have. True wisdom for a man in dire straits."

Wilson had no patience with Trevor's island attitude. "Forget it. My luck will turn."

On the front porch of the pirate-patched man's house, they were drinking rum and Coca-Cola. They were listening to ska, and the bass line was heavy. They were sampling a batch of Tobago weed that had just arrived on the island. They were respecting each other and each other's lies. Those were factors. But they were minor compared to the washing machine Wilson had so recently been sure of buying Bezi. He could face going home jobless. He could not face his wife without the money for a machine that would make her life easier.

In the morning, he woke with the sound of the surf in his ears, which was odd because the house was inland. Trevor came in with a cup of coffee. Everything that had gone wrong since Nancy first appeared at his table in the Pinnacle's dining room was there in his mind, all in one place of pain.

"What now?" Trevor wanted to know.

"I will think; I will sleep."

Trevor had his own problems. Two cruise ships were docking at the pier, and his monkey was sick. It had been throwing up green goo all night, and Trevor was haggard. Lulu was his livelihood, and he was fond of the creature.

Think. Sleep. In the course of the morning, Trevor's mother came into the room with a plateful of fried things.

That night, Lulu died. Wilson was the contagion, though they were too polite to blame him. He had brought something foul into their house. Worried, Trevor went looking for a replacement monkey.

Sleep. Think.

Days.

On the pallet, Wilson's body was going slack. He was dizzy any time he sat up. Trevor's mother kept a pitcher of fresh water and glass within easy reach. He drank but did not get up from the pallet.

After a couple of days, the vultures showed up. They had red heads and silver on the trailing edge of their wings. They found a perch in his imagination and settled in.

Trevor tried now and again to rouse him. Wilson would not be roused.

The new monkey was a male. His name was Jimmy, after Cliff. Trevor was happy again. The odor of marijuana. The odor of fish. The odor of the sea. Buzzing flies flew in one window and out another.

The morning he did get up, Wilson remembered the insult. What he had called the Turk in Jamaica. *Prairie dog*. They were in a bar in a village near Montego Bay watching television. A program about prairie dogs, and the comparison was perfect. If he had kept his mouth shut, he would not be desolate today.

Rising, he was unsteady on his legs and grabbed the edge of a table to keep from falling. He sat for a long time listening to Trevor's mother gossiping in the kitchen with a neighbor. After drinking water, he made his slow way to the kitchen.

"Lazarus," cried Trevor's mother, the great mounds of her brown flesh trembling with pleasure.

"Back from the dead," her neighbor chimed in. The neighbor's sharp-boned thinness balanced the other woman's bulk. Already they were making something for him to eat.

That afternoon he walked in the sun, scanning the sky for vultures. He had foiled them, and they were keeping their distance.

That night, he and Trevor played cards and smoked. Wilson took pleasure in the game, which they played for matchsticks. The single shot of rum he sipped created a pleasant blur of color when he closed his eyes.

"What now?" said Trevor.

Wilson shook his head.

In the morning, he picked up his suitcase and thanked Trevor's mother. He got a ride on a flatbed truck down to the harbor where the tourist shops, painted tropical colors, looked like doll houses.

He felt calm, watching people in bright clothes disembark from a cruise ship with cameras and day packs. He watched monkeys running up and down the arms and across the shoulders of the imitation Rastas, who seemed to be in a good mood. Trevor was not among them; a girlfriend took up a lot of his time.

A woman was hawking St. Kitts caps for five dollars. A man pretended to talk to someone, addressing his mobile phone as if someone were on the other end of the line. A girl with a bad foot held one end of a jump rope for a girl with braids. At a table in front of a fish restaurant, a chestnut-colored man drinking a Carib beer was explaining with his hands something intricate to a girl in a short blue skirt.

Seeing them, Wilson felt generous. Their sins, their crimes fit snugly inside his own. He was everybody's older brother, the one who had gone ahead, alone, down the road to disaster. It cost him to pull himself away. He put his hand in a pocket and came out with a little money that Trevor must have put there.

He bought a bottle of sparkling water and thought about

Bezi. He walked as though he had a destination. A cove with a thin lip of brown-sugar sand. Anchored close in was a good-sized sailboat. *El Azar, Sarasota*, was written in blue letters on the hull. A suntanned man with a hairy chest sat in the stern under an awning, reading a book. A woman in a red bikini was wading in the shallow water.

They looked at home. Wilson walked to the edge of the water, set his suitcase down, took off his shoes. The woman waved casually, and the man cupped his hands.

"Come aboard for a drink."

Wilson waded out to the sailboat. The three of them sat in the shaded stern, drinking small bottles of beer slowly. The couple were young, possibly married, surefooted.

"I'm Daphne," the woman introduced herself.

"And I'm Bill," the man said, extending a hand to shake Wilson's.

Wilson told him, "My name is Wilson Peñaranda."

Bill nodded. "We've been out for three months. Getting a little stale at this point. It's a lot of work, keeping one of these things right side up in the water. We're heading home. Sarasota. That's in Florida."

Wilson nodded. "I also am headed home. The Dominican Republic."

"Tell us something about yourself," Daphne said.

Wilson understood that he was being interviewed for a job crewing for them and that he was making a good impression.

Near the boat, a fish leaped from the sea. An eagle wheeled across the sky. Wilson had found a way home.

"Yes," said Bill. "Tell us about yourself."

"My wife's name is Bezi, and my son's name is William."

That was all there was to say. In a few minutes, he would wade ashore to get his suitcase. He would get the hang of the work as they sailed home.

IT'S A CROSSING, NOT A CRUISE

Bill Brown

Day 1

My Inside Stateroom is a windowless closet on an unfashionable lower deck of the Queen Mary 2. In the corridor outside the room, there are black and white photos hanging on the wall: images of elegant passengers in formal attire, who aren't passengers on this ship but on one of its ancestors, back when a transatlantic crossing was a big deal and an elegant affair. The photos fascinate me, at first. But then I get paranoid. Why did the masters of the ship hang those photos down here in steerage? Is it for the edification of those of us in the cheap rooms? A template for the kind of passengers we should aspire to be? Or is it to demonstrate what kind of passengers we're not, so don't bother trying?

There is a dress code on the ship. If you want to eat in the formal dining room, you have to wear a dinner jacket. I didn't bring a dinner jacket. I meant to, but I forgot. Without a jacket, I'm condemned to eat in one of the all-you-can-eat buffet restaurants or to stay in and get room service, except on those rare nights when the captain in his benevolence decides that dinner will be informal. It's just as well. In the formal dining room, you share a table with other people, usually older retired couples, and no one likes to share a table with a youngish solo guy (me). Older gentlemen who travel alone are generally considered endearingly tragic ("I hear his wife keeled over last year at the Winnipeg Curling Club Invitational") or colorful ("He makes the cha-cha look like dirty dancing"), and they like to spin yarns (an old nautical term, by the way, that has to do with rope making). But younger solo travelers are sketchy and suspect because what kind of youngish guy is traveling alone on a fancy cruise ship? In an

Agatha Christie novel, that's the guy everyone would think is the killer till the real killer tosses him overboard.

The cheap rooms don't have windows. Instead, I have a TV that I can tune to channel 38, which is a live feed from a video camera located on the bridge. This evening, channel 38 is broadcasting a view of the English Channel. France plays a supporting role. It is a dark, uneven line in the distance. After a while, the line gets finer and fainter: from a Sharpie marker to a felt tip pen, to a sharp gray pencil. Then the line vanishes, and there's just the strict geometry of sky and sea. Since I'm a landlubber who likes old Westerns, my current situation conjures up images of covered wagons crossing the desert, only this covered wagon has art history lectures, a restaurant that can seat 1200 people, a health spa, a cigar bar, and showgirls.

I'm crossing the Atlantic on the QM2 not because I'm a fan of cruises or the ridiculous anglophilia of the Cunard Line or wearing a tuxedo and dancing to ABBA in 30-foot swells, but because, at this point in my life, I've given up on flying. I am crossing from the UK to the USA by sea, and I am alone.

As the days pass, I begin to notice two categories of solo travelers: the Flamboyantly Solo and the Discreetly Alone. The former advertise their solo status and enthusiastically participate in group activities, which on the QM2 include competitive darts and a talent show that I decide to attend for the LOLs, but which just leaves me stricken by the poignancy of human existence. Some of the Flamboyantly Solo passengers eventually hook up with one another and graduate to the status of Conspicuously Coupled. Flamboyantly Solo travelers thus seem to enjoy the cruise life, but Discreetly Alone passengers do not. They eat alone and keep to themselves. Eventually, we Discreet Loners begin to notice each other, sitting in dark corners with a book or wandering some unpeopled stretch of an upper deck. We exchange barely perceptible nods and wonder what's the deal with each other.

At dinner, I order room service. It's a nice perk. On a cruise ship, food comes with the price of your ticket, and even room service is included. I ask for a bowl of tomato soup and a slice of apple pie. It's buffet food, but when it arrives on a rolling table covered with white linen, it seems fancier than that. Each plate is covered with a silver cloche, so getting to your food is like opening birthday presents, one by one, each plate like a little surprise.

Day 2

Before I embark, my girlfriend asks me if I've read David Foster Wallace's essay "A Supposedly Fun Thing I'll Never Do Again," about the time Wallace took a Caribbean cruise and basically hated it. I tell her that yes, I've read it, but this isn't that kind of ship. In fact, everyone on the QM2 makes a big deal about the fact that the QM2 isn't a cruise ship, it's an Ocean Liner, and that this isn't a cruise, it's a Crossing, i.e., we're crossing the Atlantic. But it's more than just a matter of semantics. As far as the passengers of the QM2 are concerned, a cruise is a journey to nowhere that cheesy people take to get sunburned and do jello shots and skinny dip in a hot tub, while a crossing is serious business. It's got purpose, and besides that, it's classy. So please don't call it a cruise, and don't bother ordering a jello shot because you can't get one.

Tonight is another formal night. I order room service again and stare at the TV, trying to decipher Hollywood movies dubbed into French. I find a glossy magazine in the top desk drawer. It's a lifestyle travel magazine with articles about wine tours in Tuscany and the best hotels on the French Riviera. There are photos of the Queen Mary 2, as well. It's the usual spread: older guys in tuxedos and ladies hanging on their arms in glittering gowns. There's usually a waiter hovering nearby, too, pouring these people champagne or presenting them with a tray of hors d'oeuvres. It's not just this travel magazine, either. You see images like that plastered all over the ship. Pictures of generally famous dead people getting waited on. That's the QM2's brand. You are here to be pampered by people who are paid to pamper you. Never mind that you don't actually get pampered like that, let alone hobnob with celebs unless you're one of the ballers on the upper decks who eat in their own private restaurants and are attended to by their own private staff.

Of course, these glossy spreads don't spend any time on the real price of all this pampering. No mention of where the people who are pampering you come from (Central America, Eastern Europe, Southeast Asia; Filipinos represent the largest single nationality on most cruise lines), or what their schedule is like (12 hours a day, sometimes more, 7 days a week), or whether they have job security (no), or how long it's been since they've seen their families (8-10 months for a standard employment contract, usually).

Day 3

I find the cappuccino. There's a machine at one of the bars on Deck 7. It's pretty good, but you have to pay extra for it. That's the genius of the business model. There are miles of buffet trays and bottomless urns of coffee on this ship, but if you want to go à la carte, you have to cough up the cash.

After I get my coffee, I grab a fruit plate from the breakfast buffet. I leave my tray unattended for a second to grab some OJ when some kind of senior officer gripes at me.

"Don't leave your food lying around," he barks in a slightly toned-down version of the voice he uses to browbeat the boatswain or whoever.

"Sorry," I say.

"It's not for me. It's for you," he continues. "If you leave it lying around, all sorts of people will breathe on it."

I frown because a. this guy is annoying, and b. I'm not so sure about his version of germ theory. I want to tell him to stick to sailing the boat, but I don't say anything at all. I just feel sorry for all the crew people who have to work for the jerk.

This encounter gets me thinking about mutiny and whether it's something that sailors still do, especially sailors on a luxury cruise ship. I mean, who could blame them? Aside from the occasional "passenger mutiny" when a group of preternaturally un-self-aware passengers scream at the captain because they're dissatisfied with their Zumba classes, the Internet is mostly silent on the matter of mutiny, though an incident on a Carnival Cruise Lines ship in 1981 is probably emblematic. The ship was docked in Miami when the crew, mostly workers from Central America, went on strike over labor issues. Carnival promptly broke the strike by calling the American immigration cops, who arrested the striking crew, declared them undocumented immigrants, and deported them.

Day 4

I'm reading a book about America written by Bernard-Henri Lévy. Lévy is a French celebrity intellectual, which is a category of celebrity that is unheard of in the U.S. where celebrities are seldom expected to have an opinion one way or another about the teleology of consciousness. The book is not flattering. Lévy writes about American megamalls, NASCAR racing, 9/11 hysteria, and fast-food restaurants, which he describes as "franchised feeding machines." It's not a good book to read when you're on a ship heading to the USA, and there's no turning back, let alone hopping off midway.

I decide that I should put aside the celebrity intellectual's manual on how crappy America is, and I should get out of my cabin, and I should do something. So, I sign up for a wine tasting. The chief sommelier is a Canadian guy with beady eyes and a big booming voice who confides that he formed his tasting palate by drinking Big Gulps at 7-11 after hockey practice in Saskatoon. He breaks out four wines, two from the Old World, two from the New. One of the New World wines is from Australia, which I'd never thought of before as the New World since I thought the US had a lock on that brand. But of course, it is another version of the New World, a place where disgruntled Old Worlders fled to or were unwillingly dumped.

"Old World wine asks a question," the Canadian sommelier expounds, "while New World wine gives an answer."

It's a pithy statement that seems worth trying to apply recklessly to the difference between Europeans and Americans in general.

During the wine tasting, I sit between a guy from Baltimore who is returning from 5 years in Zambia as a missionary and a Spanish lady who is accompanied by her grumpy boyfriend. The Canadian sommelier talks about terroir and rim-to-core ratios, all very interesting, but I'm focused on the cheese plate that the missionary guy is hogging ("You can't get cheese like this in Zambia," he mumbles with his mouth full). After we taste the four wines, the assistant sommelier- Francesco- breaks out a mystery wine and asks the chief sommelier to figure out what it is. The chief takes a sip. Then he furrows his brow.

"Let me sit down. I have to let this wine speak to me."

He sits down. But the wine seems to be giving him the silent treatment. The chief sommelier asks Francesco for a hint, but Francesco just smiles and shrugs and seems to be enjoying the fact that he is publicly humiliating his boss.

Day 5

I wake up and head to breakfast. Out in the corridor, one of the housekeepers is maneuvering a monster cart stacked high with bath towels and toilet paper through a side door. The hallway is narrow, and the geometry is all wrong, so it takes her a while, moving back and forth, like when you're trying to get out of a particularly tight parallel parking space. Finally, she shoves the cart through a door with a "Staff Only" sign affixed to it.

It's a door that separates the ships backstage from the front of house. On this side of the door, the ship is a theatrical production complete with fiberglass Art Deco details, evening dress-up, and black-and-white poster prints of Bing Crosby smoking his pipe on some long-ago transatlantic voyage. Everything feels unreal, glossed over with promotional copy, and surrounded by quotation marks. But on the other side of the door, there's a real ship where people work long hours washing the linen napkins and recycling the champagne bottles.

I read that after it was retired from service back in the 1970s, the QM2's predecessor, the Queen Mary, was permanently anchored in Long Beach, California. It's been there ever since, converted into a hotel and a roadside attraction. If you want, you can spend the night in one of the old staterooms and play shuffleboard on deck, then dine at Sir Winston's Restaurant or the Chelsea Chowder House. There are even ghost tours (the Queen Mary has been voted one of the "Top 10 Most Haunted Places in America" by *Time* Magazine). It occurs to me that the ship I'm on might, one day, meet a similar fate. Then it occurs to me that, aside from the whole sailing across the ocean thing, it already has.

My favorite place to spend the day is on the lowest deck, at least the lowest one I can get to as a passenger. There's a long corridor down there with a row of card tables topped with green felt. The tables sit next to big windows that are just above the waterline. Down here, the ocean is close by, a surge of slate-gray and seaweed-green flecked with white froth. A crazy, swelling, pulsing thing that I'm separated from by just an inch or two of glass.

A couple guys are sitting at one of the card tables writing a song for the songwriting workshop that's being run by Chris Difford, one of the founding members of the British band Squeeze. In high school, I bought their second album "Cool for Cats" on cassette tape, and even today, if I hear any of the songs,

I'm instantly transported back to that time in my life and how I felt back then, which was generally miserable. I don't know why a guy from Squeeze was invited to the QM2, considering the entertainment is aimed at a much older crowd. On this voyage, it includes the 9-piece Royal Court Theater Orchestra, as well as a lavish musical production called "Viva Italia."

"Excuse me," one of the songwriters who looks about my age says to me. "Could you tell us what you think of our song?"

"Sure," I say.

The guy who talked to me starts to play some blues chords on his acoustic guitar while the other guy sings. The lyrics are about the Internet, including a memorable one that goes, "I've got the heartache crashing, keyboard smashing, social network blues."

After the guys finish, they ask me what I think of the song. "I like it," I say. "What's it about?"

"It's a love song about Facebook," the guitarist says.

Day 6

Somewhere on the high seas east of Boston. I'm standing on deck early in the morning with a few of the other Discreet Loners. We're all staring at our cell phones. In pirate movies, there's always a scene where a pirate scrambles up the mainmast and perches in the crow's nest with a spyglass, ready to call out at the first glimpse of some faraway shore. But now, it's passengers on the promenade deck of a cruise ship holding their cell phones in the air and waiting for reception.

Finally, after six long days at sea, the first short bar of a cell phone signal pops up in the corner of my screen.

"Land Ho!" I call out to no one in particular.

AN ENGLISHMAN IN CONSTANTINOPLE

James Gallant

In the summer of 1595, Thomas Dallam was bound for Constantinople. He reached Venice aboard the ship *Hector* that was transporting Queen Elizabeth's gift to the new Sultan, Muhammad III: the "clock-organ" Dallam had invented: a complex apparatus with a number of moving parts that could either be played manually or set to run through a repertoire of mechanized performances at a specific hour.

Dallam arrived in Venice after dark. A limping dwarf appeared, a lantern swinging from one hand, and conducted him to a gondolier who, Dallam was told, would carry him to an inn.

The wide, dark Grand Canal mirrored a million stars. Only the slap of the boatman's oar in the black water broke the silence. Dallam looked to the palaces in the distance, silhouetted by starlight, for reassurance that he was still on Earth and not being conveyed to Hades by Charon.

The gondola exited the Grand Canal into narrower channels winding between buildings under short, arched bridges. Venice was notorious for skullduggery, and Dallam had no idea where he was being taken. Did the gondolier assume his leather valise held valuables? Many of the buildings they passed appeared to be residences, but their windows were dark. If he were to cry out for help, who would hear? He prayed silently, pledging improved future behavior in exchange for present salvation.

The gondola went around yet another bend, under another short bridge, and then bumped gently against the foot of a stairway leading up to a door illuminated by a small, flickering gas lamp. The boatman indicated that Dallam should follow him.

Dallam refused.

The boatman shrugged, climbed the stairs himself, and

pounded the metal knocker on the door. A man in a nightshirt appeared, candlestick in hand. The boatman pointed to Dallam. There was a mumbled conversation, an exchange of laughter, then the man in the nightshirt called down to Dallam, "Osteria! Osteria!"—inn—gesturing for him to ascend the stairs.

Dallam needed a place to stay the night and would have to trust someone, so he rose the steps reluctantly.

———— ✦ ————

Upon rising the next morning, he discovered that repairs were necessary to the *Hector*. There would be a delay in its departure to Constantinople. This was not entirely unwelcome since he had already been at sea a month. He became a tourist impromptu.

He had supposed transportation in watery Venice was solely by the canals but discovered one could be a pedestrian there. He made long rambles along narrow streets and alleys and over small bridges linking neighborhoods organized around small central squares and fountains. Great wealth and grinding poverty were curiously juxtaposed, but class distinctions seemed as fluid as the environment: cobblers' and tailors' wives wore silk gowns with silver buttons and might have attendants carrying the luxurious long trains of their dresses. Noble women and merchants' wives wore *chopines*: platform shoes that might elevate a woman a foot off the ground. The transparent black veils women wore, which extended from the top of the head nearly to the feet, did not obscure their being bare-breasted, and Dallam started at the sight of a shapely, smiling woman striding toward him smiling who, beneath her veil, was clearly completely naked.

In England, he had acquired the impression Jews were a dirty, rapacious people but found those attending the Saturday service in a ghetto synagogue clean and dignified. The congregation sat in a circle while the rabbi read from and commented upon the five books of Moses. They sang Psalms as the English did in church, and Dallam appreciated the absence of Popish images about the synagogue. As far as he could see, the only error of the

Jews was their failure to accept Christ as their Lord and Savior.

In the yard of an old monastery chapel, he observed what he took at first to be a pile of stone rubble before realizing the contents were, in fact, shattered human skulls and bones. A nun from the convent adjacent to the chapel explained that the bones were those of friars buried centuries ago in a field nearby. The bones had been unearthed during excavations preparatory to constructing a home for sick and indigent women.

That the friars, whose corruption had been legendary, should end up so seemed entirely just.

The Church of the Apostles was an abhorrent reminder of the Romish religion. Freestanding statues of eight apostles roosted atop the Church. Four more—James, Peter, Paul, and Matthew—occupied niches in the façade. The church interior was all shadows and mystery, with small oil lamps illuminating the shrines of saints, the scent of candlewax and incense, and the droning and mumming of priests. Poor, deluded Venetians knelt before a doll of Mary and kissed it.

—————— ✦ ——————

Dallam was on his way to Constantinople when his ship met with strong winds, booming thunder, and lightning in the Sea of Crete. A friar who was on board asserted that such violence in the heavens could only be an expression of Divine Wrath. He urged prayers to Our Lady and St. Mark and a group singing of "Salve Regina" and "Ave Maria," and he circulated among the passengers and crew an image of Mary to be kissed.

Dallam refused participation in these superstitions and informed the crew and passengers that one who prays to any person other than God the Father, or his only begotten Son, deprives them of the honor due them.

The storms had continued for three days when suspicion grew among the passengers and crew that the heretical Englishman was the source of Divine displeasure. There was talk of heaving him overboard.

"I am a Christian, as you profess to be," Dallam protested. "That I am a sinner, I freely acknowledge, but before you ascribe our difficulties to me, should you not ponder your own worthiness?"

The friar concurred. "Let he who is without sin among you cast the first stone."

———— ✦ ————

When Dallam reached Constantinople, rather than proceeding directly to the Sultan's palace, he ordered the crates containing the unassembled parts of the clock-organ delivered to the residence of English ambassador Lollo, where he was to stay.

He was glad that he had done so because he discovered when he opened the crates containing the components of the clock-organ that intense heat in the ship's hold had melted glues in cabinet joints which would have to be rejoined.

Dallam, a slender fellow in his late twenties, haggard after months at sea, looked with the eyes of a lover upon the beef, deer, and veal Lollo's servants placed before him.

"I should warn you about the reception you may expect from Mehmet," Lollo said. "If he were a Christian ruler, you could anticipate expressions of gratitude for the Queen's gift, but he will regard it as a suitable expression of obeisance."

"Well, a turd in his teeth!"

Lollo smiled. "The emotion you express, I have experienced often enough here. I will give you an example. Dwarfs armed with scimitars guard the royal palace. I've been through the palace gate often enough to be thoroughly familiar to those fellows—I know their names. I am nonetheless searched for weapons and poisons every time I arrive. And before I speak with Sultan, I must first kiss his knee or sleeve. Oh, and by the way, when one leaves his presence, one never shows to His Majesty one's backside."

"Well, how *does* one leave?"

"One backs away from him."

Dallam was laughing.

"Yes, it's all quite silly, but your life may depend on honoring these formalities. Human life here is more disposable than we are accustomed to regarding it in England."

Dallam frowned.

"Mehmet, for his amusement, will sometimes have mentally deficient persons thrown down wells. He enjoys hearing their echoing screams. After he became Emperor recently, he executed nineteen of his brothers."

"The heathen whoreson! *Why?*"

"He wished to eliminate any possible competition."

"Elizabeth curries favor with this ditch dog?"

"It's just politics. The Turks are as hostile to Spain and the Pope as we are. Mehmet once asked me whether Elizabeth could be induced to join forces with him, conquer Spain, and divide the country between them. I mentioned it to Elizabeth."

"What'd she say?"

"Nothing."

Lollo's servant placed before the two men small bowls of something yellow topped with almonds.

"What is it?" Dallam asked.

"*Zerde.* Rice boiled in honey water."

Dallam had a taste. Not bad, although he preferred cake.

———— ✦ ————

Dallam's order from the palace was to install the clock-organ in a spacious domed hall on an elevated platform. Dallam did this, tested his invention, and announced its readiness for the Sultan's inspection.

He was informed that he was not to be on the platform when the Sultan appeared but in a small adjacent closet. Dallam nearly asked *why* before remembering Lollo's admonition that he must never ever do this. He set the timer on the organ so it would start running through its scheduled performances shortly after the Sultan entered the hall.

Seated on a stool in the dark closet, Dallam heard the trumpets' fanfare, the birds' twittering, the contrapuntal melodies. From there, he was attended by a guard, and when it did sixteen bells, he knew, without having to see, that the miniature blackbirds and thrushes in the holly bush atop the organ were flapping their wings and that the Queen Elizabeth doll had raised her scepter magisterially.

A guard opened the door. Dallam blinked at the rush of bright light from the hall.

"The Sultan had enjoyed very much the performance and wishes to know when it will be repeated."

"It will be repeated automatically in an hour," Dallam explained. "However, one can start it at any time by depressing the small lever to the left of the keyboard."

The guard shut the door but reappeared again shortly. "The Sultan cannot find the lever you mentioned. He would like you to show it to him and perform on the organ."

Dallam stepped out into the light. The Sultan sat on the platform some five yards distant, looking over his shoulder at Dallam, bushy eyebrows arched in what seemed an expression of disdain. He had a goatee and winged mustachios and wore an immense turban with a golden crown perched on top.

A crowd of uniformed men filled the hall below the platform. There were perhaps a hundred yellow-gowned pages with identical shaved heads and locks of hair hanging down behind their ears like squirrel's tails. Another company of men had hawks perched on gloved wrists, and there was a phalanx of dwarfs, each with his long scimitar buckler.

"The Sultan orders you to approach and play upon the organ," the guard said.

Dallam hesitated. "If I did that, I would have to turn my back on the Sultan."

The guard conferred with the Sultan and returned with word that Dallam would enjoy a special dispensation to turn his back on the Emperor while performing.

Dallam approached the Sultan and bowed. The Sultan nodded slightly in response.

Seated at the organ, Dallam played "Greensleeves" as best he could with trembling hands. The Sultan, seeking a better view of what the performer's hands were doing, rose from his seat and bumped the back of Dallam's head lightly, inspiring the organist to wonder if, owing to some unknown violation of protocol, his neck was about to be separated from his body.

Dallam pressed the lever that set the mechanism going again. The Sultan appeared happy as a child with a new toy, and when the automated performance had concluded, he handed Dallam a leather pouch containing forty-five pieces of gold.

—— ✦ ——

A counselor to Mehmet appeared at the ambassador's house to express the Emperor's great satisfaction with the clock-organ and to order Dallam to remain in the city and fashion other equally clever devices.

"I must soon return to my family in England," said Dallam, who was not married.

"That will not be possible," the counselor said. "Come with me."

He led Dallam to the palace, through adjoining courtyards, and onto the parapet overlooking sunken baths filled with naked young women.

"The women are all white," Dallam observed.

"Slave women from the Caucasus," the counselor explained. "You may have any three you like and an apartment at the palace in which to enjoy them."

Dallam, pretending acceptance of Sultan's command, was given leave to return to the English ambassador's home and gather his personal possessions.

With Lollo's assistance, Dallam contacted an English merchant from Lancashire, an exporter with offices in Constantinople, whose servant led Dallam after dark to a point along the Greek border from which escape from the Ottoman Empire was possible, and from there, Dallam was able to make his way back to London, which he vowed never to leave again.

A SHIP OF DREAMS

Kathy Dunkerley

Good parents, I believe, can be characterized by a selfless devotion to their children's happiness and well-being. However, I am sure there are limits as to how far we should pander to every whim and desire expressed by our offspring. After all, no parent wants to raise an overindulged child who melts like a popsicle in the sun every time he or she does not get their way.

But there are times when you have no choice but to give in to your child, even when your instincts are screaming no. No. A thousand times, no. A case in point was when my youngest daughter Annie and I saw an advert for a Disney Cruise, which promised turquoise water, wide sandy beaches, and a cast of shipmates ranging from Mickey Mouse to that most roguish of pirates, Captain Jack Sparrow.

Annie turned to me once the advert was finished. "Mummy, please, please, please," she said, and her tiny, high-pitched voice quivered with excitement. "I want to see Mickey. Belle. Elsa. She's my favorite."

I could see the longing that gleamed in her baby-blue eyes and knew it would be impossible to say no. After all, my child would have the time of her life, and I could float lazily over the peacock blue sea and drink icy cocktails as tropical breezes caress my skin.

So, with a heavy heart and more than a little trepidation, I stand on the dock in the Port of Miami, waiting to board the Disney Dream, which I was assured is the flagship liner in the Disney Fleet. As usual, Miami is hot and muggy, and in the thick, soupy, sticky air, it feels like I'm entombed in treacle. I brush away the beads of sweat that bubble on my brow and stare at the giant ship, which to me looks more like a 10-story block of flats. The Dream sits solidly in the murky grey water, which is surprising as I had visions of a ship that serenely floats over an absurdly blue sea. But what do you expect in a busy seaport, I console myself. Surely after the ship sets sail, the air will no longer smell like rotten eggs, and the oil slicks that pool on the surface of the opaque water will disappear. It suddenly occurs to me that the ship looks top-heavy, as if it could topple in the faintest breeze. Wasn't there a hurricane that flattened Florida not long ago? Even in the hot, humid air, I shiver.

"Mummy," my daughter says and pulls on my arm. "Do you see Mickey?" She points to the two chimney stacks perched on the top of the ship. Each of the chimneys is painted a gaudy, bright red color, contrasting with the dazzling, iridescent white paint covering the boat's top half. Instinctively, I reach into my bag for my sunglasses.

"Mummy," Annie says, her voice shrill as the gulls that cry mournfully in the cloudless sky. For a moment, there is a whiff of a salty breeze, which ruffles my hair, and I sniff the salty, sulphury smell of seaweed. I am immediately reminded of the seashore where we took Annie last year. It was nice to have the damp sand squidge between our toes, feel the summer sun kiss our skin, and hear the waves as they lapped the shoreline. Yes, maybe the cruise will be all right after all.

"There's Mickey, Mummy," Annie says, pointing to huge images of the world's most famous mouse. To be honest, until then, I hadn't noticed that gigantic versions of Mickey Mouse's face were painted onto the smokestacks' scarlet surfaces.

I can't believe we are already bombarded with images of Disney cartoons, and I haven't even boarded the ship yet. I groan.

"Mummy," Annie says, staring at my face, which I know is red from the heat and probably streaked with black, non-waterproof mascara. "Are you upset, Mummy? Did you eat something funny at breakfast?"

"No darling," I say and grasp her little hand in mine, but to be honest, at this point, our hands are so shiny with sweat that her slippery fist seems to slide from my grip.

"Mummy." I grab my little Annie's hand tighter, grit my teeth, and we make our way to the check-in desks, which line the far end of the departure hall, and a row of earnest, eager check-in assistants vie for the honor of checking us in. It is not long until we board the ship and enter the vast atrium, which seems to soar upwards toward the upper floors of the ship. I look up at a huge scraggly object which looks somewhat like a tree. I touch its surface, which has the texture of the bucket and spade we gave Annie on last year's beach holiday. Plastic. I remove my hand quickly as if I'd been scalded by the polyurethane surface. Then I look up and see the branches of this so-called tree are covered with pumpkins. Well, jack-o-lanterns, really, and each is carved with a grim, repellent face. But wait a minute, I think, pumpkins don't grow on trees, and then I notice that the pumpkins are made of orange-colored cardboard. You have to wonder how Disney can get away from this massive deviation from reality.

Then I hear it. The loud, cacophonous noise sounds like hundreds of piercing, high-pitched squeals. What could it be? I look down at little Annie. She has frantic spots of color on each of her freckled cheeks, and her eyes, which are round as dinner plates, gleam with happiness and joy.

"Annie. Are you all right? It's awfully loud in here."

Suddenly, Annie opens her mouth and screams at the top of her lungs, and her own shrieks join the hyperactive voices of what must be at least a thousand small children who swarm over this large open space.

"Mickey," all the children cry, almost in unison, and when I look up, I see a large, life-sized mouse with huge black rounded ears and a strange pointy nose. He is, I see, dressed in nautically appropriate garb, which consists of a blue, double-breasted jacket with rows of brass buttons down the front. Between his oversized ears sits a round white hat with a black brim looped with a row of shiny gold braid. Is Mickey Mouse actually going to captain this ship?

"It's Mickey, Mummy," and then the mouse reaches down and takes my daughter's hand. I stifle a laugh when I realize Mickey and Annie share the very same squeaky tones, which to me sound very much like fingernails on a blackboard. But then I glance at Annie, who stares adoringly at this depiction of a mouse, and know that my opinion will count very little here. Oh well. When Mickey walks off to enchant some other small child, I take Annie's hand, which in the air-conditioned air seems to have lost its slippery, sweaty texture.

"Mummy." I follow Annie's eyes, which are fixed on a young woman with plastic-looking, thick mahogany-colored hair. She is dressed in a tiered floor-length dress fashioned into layers of bright yellow ruffles. The dress looks like a blancmange, that sweet, elegantly molded pudding that always looks better than it tastes. Oh well.

"It's Belle," Annie cries. "You know Beauty and the Beast."

My daughter is literally shaking with excitement. I can't help myself, and I reach out to touch the yellow dress's shiny fabric, and to me, the slithery surface feels like the tawdry, polyester curtains that draped the windows in my first halls of residence. The young woman glares at me, and I quickly remove my hand. Belle, to her credit, quickly regains her composure and beams down at Annie, who stares up at this Disney character with an enraptured look on her face. Although I cannot completely understand why, it's obvious my daughter has fallen in love with Belle, a pretend Disney character with plastic hair dressed in a garish, polyethylene frock.

The young woman moves off, and I take Annie's hand once again. "It's time to see our room," I say. I smile down at her and see her face creased with a huge smile, which splits her chubby face practically in two. "Would you like that?" I say.

She nods, and we head towards the throngs of men, women, and children crammed tightly together in front of elevators that will take us to our staterooms. After an interminable wait, we squeeze onto the overcrowded lift, and eventually, the blinking neon lights indicate we've managed to reach the 10th floor. We soon emerge onto the long, windy, red-carpeted corridor that leads to our cabin. We stop momentarily, and I kneel, tilt Annie's chin, and watch her blue eyes dance in her pink, flushed face.

"Mummy," she says again.

I smile.

"Yes, dear?"

"This is just going to be the most fun we've ever had," she says.

I feel my back teeth clench, but I ignore the twinge that travels up my jaw.

"We certainly are, darling."

I grasp her small hand, and we head for our room.

BUT NOT THE SCREAM

Adam Berlin

The pilot says we're starting our approach, expect turbulence, there's a storm, and right before plane touches runway, KLM, the connection from Amsterdam, a gust pushes us too left. The pilot pulls us back, or the GPS or ILS, or another gust, and everyone applauds when the braking ends, not the way Europeans applaud landings but from making it down after danger, a story to tell, the time they landed in Bergen during Storm Hans (big enough to get a name).

Bergen's got too many tourists. After the Munch museum, the famous one's not there, and cinnamon rolls, Norway supposedly famous for its cinnamon rolls (they're too dry), we're drenched, ready to go.

In the morning, we pick up the Peugeot from Sixt rent a car (my tip to travelers: rent compact), and we're off—to Voss, to Loen, to Aurland, to Stranda. We drive up mountains, down mountains, through mountains, around fjords, and feel the away we wanted. A few cars, a few tour buses, but mostly super-tall trucks, headlights too high/too bright in tunnels, tunnel after tunnel, some 26 km long (in 1, I make a U-turn after a wrong turn, and my son loves that—he's 7) (saves us 25 km). My son swims in a fjord for less than a minute—2 jump-ins, too cold. We eat salmon and smoked salmon. We hike in mud (Storm Hans). We ride gondolas. We sneak onto 1 gondola at night. I tell my kid: Sometimes you need to break some rules. The guy who runs the lift is cool; end of shift, lets us on. We go up, go down, town and lake and mountains like a movie, wide-angle to almost close-up. 1 morning, my son skips his first stones. Some roads stop at ferry crossings. We drive on, get out of the car, look, get back in the car, drive off.

Rauma looks end-of-the-world. Rocks, wind, cold. Everything feels like jutting sounds. We drive down/up Trollstigen.

We pretend adventure, but it is too. The storm. The tunnels. The hairpin roads. The paintings that show faces ready to scream (but not The Scream).

Our last night's in Osterbo. No one's around except campers and staff, and the salmon's good, and we hike. 2 sheep run away when we're too close. I say: Is it something we said? Katherine jumps rock to rock gracefully. Eben smashes wide yellow mushrooms.

We drive back to Bergen. We're flying to Copenhagen next. We'll rent bikes and visit The Little Mermaid, but we already know: The Little Mermaid will be too crowded, like the room with the Mona Lisa. The statue will be okay (like the painting's smile's okay), but it's a check mark, a picture to take without looking; so many people taking pictures, everyone's shot will have people taking pictures.

A CONVERSATION WITH ADAM BERLIN

Lowestoft Chronicle Interview by Nicholas Litchfield
(June 2024)

Adam Berlin
(Photography: Jeffrey Heiman)

More than two decades ago, writer Adam Berlin found success with his first book, earning a starred review from *Booklist* (which called it "A powerful debut novel with fascinating characters") and favorable remarks in *The New York Times*. His subsequent book drew more critical raves, with periodicals like *Publisher's Weekly* observing, "Berlin displays a nice, quirky sense of dialogue, and his violent scenes are etched with convincing—if sometimes gruesome—detail." That novel was ultimately awarded the Ferro-Grumley Award for the year's best LGBT fiction and was optioned for film.

Over the years, Berlin has received further literary awards, including The Clay Reynolds Novella Prize and, most recently, the Tartts Fiction Award. The prize comprises publication via Livingston Press at the University of West Alabama and marks Berlin's debut short story collection.

In this exclusive interview with *Lowestoft Chronicle*, Berlin discusses his writing career, the backstory to his early novels, his first literary agent, and some of the stories in his newly published fiction collection.

Lowestoft Chronicle (LC): Since 1991, dozens of your stories have appeared in literary journals like *The Greensboro Review* and *New Delta Review*. Interestingly, *All Around They're Taking Down the Lights*, published in August, is your first story collection, and it's mostly comprised of newer fiction. What motivated this collection, and why release one now and not, say, twenty years ago, when *Belmondo Style* was garnering high praise?

Adam Berlin (AB): While I've published many stories since I received my MFA from Brooklyn College, several in *All Around They're Taking Down the Lights* are more recently written. As for publication, I sent out different iterations of the current collection, but I finally found the right mix between chronological order (the first story is about a college kid, and the last is about a tenured prof.) and thematic throughline (the male narrator in each story behaves badly on the way to becoming a more-layered man). The collection's epigraph is a James Dean quote, "Being a good actor isn't easy. Being a man is even harder. I want to be both before I'm done." The dynamic of living up to male tropes, often established by Hollywood leading bad boys, and the recognition that these tropes have damaging and damage-inducing edges ground my collection. When I sent out this line-up of stories, I was thrilled when Joe Taylor at Livingston Press gave my collection a home.

I did think *Belmondo Style*, my second novel on the heels of *Headlock*, my first, was going to be my early ticket to a wider readership and immediate book contracts, including a contract for a story collection. It wasn't. I won a pretty big award—The Publishing Triangle's Ferro-Grumley Award for best gay-themed novel—but the novel didn't sell as well as St. Martin's had hoped. The hard fact is that literary fiction is a tough sell, especially story collections. I'm very pleased, after many years, that my first collection is finally out there.

LC: The title of the book stems from the story "Extra," where a background actor yearns for a spark of insight that might further his career. Other stories, such as "Picasso's Model," have a fair number of indelible sentences. What made you choose this title?

AB: "Extra" is one of my flash pieces interspersed between stories—the collection has five flash pieces and ten full-length stories. I wanted a title for the collection that pointed to how Hollywood dreams diminish with time and felt *All Around They're Taking Down the Lights* suggested this kind of entropy. The spotlights that shine on us in youth (optimism, the feeling that we can do anything, and, specific to my collection, that we can live movie moments without repercussions) become less bright. There's something depressing about this inevitable dimming, but there's also something necessary, even redeeming. We grow up by growing past our youthful needs, or dreams, or obsessions. A big part of the Hollywood dream is superficial— that's why James Dean recognized the goal of becoming a good man was even harder. He understood, and I think my characters understand, that there's a place for the look-at-me-for-what-I look-like definition of men and movie stars (what the actor in my flash piece "Extra" wants, even if, as the title says, he's just an extra), but that the more nuanced look-at-me-for-who-I-am definition holds more weight and is more admirable. This ties into being a better man, I think. For the actor/narrator in "Extra," he realizes his time is done—he can stare down the leading man, the one who has made it, and that gives him momentary power, a physical assertion of look-at-me, but it's mostly worthless power. So, the lights on the characters in my collection are dimming on certain dreams, with hints that better dreams, more realistic dreams, more grounded dreams can emerge.

There's another side to the title as well. The Hollywood ideal of men has changed. The leading men from before my (and my characters') time, and the leading men the characters in my collection admire, like James Dean with his red leather jacket, and Marlon Brando with his motorcycle-swagger, and Jean-Paul Belmondo with his macho-cool and ex-boxer's confidence, are dated. There's an element of wanna-be in my male characters that gets them in trouble, but there's also something lost when their alpha gets blunted. As the stories progress and, ideally, build on each other, and as my characters recognize they should move beyond their leading-man ideals, there's a sense of loss, too. Technicolor times become less vibrant. The irreverent, fuck-it highs that happen during the movie-star moments in my characters' lives become less intense.

I think we've all had those moments when we've felt the spotlight right there, shining right on us—moments solidified and even brightened by memory, moments that often define us. We were movie stars for a moment, but those moments are impossible to sustain and become rarer, I think, as we grow up.

LC: Given that this is a collection about men and movies and "the underside of trying to live up to male tropes," recent stories like "Like they teach in acting class" from the literary journal *BODY* seem an appropriate fit. How did you decide what pieces to include and what to cut? Will some of those earlier stories be part of a future collection?

AB: Thank you for doing such a deep dive into my work, Nicholas. Yes, the flash piece in *BODY* has a thematic connection to the collection. I felt this piece would be somewhat redundant when placed near some of the other flash pieces, so I kept it out. Most of the stories I've written, all of them, really, are about men struggling (often against their self-destructive male tendencies), so there was a lot I left out. As I said, I had many iterations of a story collection before I settled on this collection. And, yes, I'm thinking of putting together a second collection. The stories in

All Around They're Taking Down the Lights are mostly about single men with few responsibilities, which makes it easier for them to pretend Hollywood. I'm now married to a special woman, and we're parents to a young son, so my feelings about being a "better" man have shifted, and this shift has, of course, entered my writing. Before I met my wife, I led a fast life, often irresponsible, sometimes seedy, full of excess, much like my characters in *All Around*. When I have enough stories for a second collection and when I find a clear throughline to order the pieces, I'll start sending out the work. Perhaps Livingston Press will be interested in a companion collection.

LC: "Ten," "Romance of the Seas," and other deftly worked pieces explore self-esteem, and writing slumps, and even the challenges of teaching. There's a tough, masculine swagger to the prose and a sharp, provocative edge to the dialogue. Naturally, at times, the light casts an ugly shadow on some of the narrators. Was this a conscious decision to focus on inglorious types? Or, as author Steve Almond more fittingly describes them, "bruised dreamers searching for a better shake in things and often losing their grip."

AB: Steve Almond, a writer I greatly admire, was kind enough to provide a blurb for my collection, and his line is fitting. There is an ugly shadow cast by many of my narrators—they're not only bruised but bruising, often irresponsibly so, which adds to their ugliness. When men swagger, a physical show of assertion, of taking up space, of saying with their bodies, "Look at me," they often hit and hurt people in their way. But as with my title, there are layers to walking this way (and all it means), and sometimes, a swagger can give power to people in the swaggerer's path. In one story titled "Black Belt," a newly divorced man who is about to get evicted from his apartment poses as a karate teacher and helps an autistic boy find some self-confidence. What starts as a cynical way to make a few bucks moves to a deep connection—a better-man moment and perhaps the most uplifting moment in the collection. In another story, "A Picture of You," a woman re-establishes her independence when the narrator's narcissism crosses a condescending line. As for "Ten" and "Romance of the Seas," the narrators are writers who aren't living up to their writing dreams. Here, I stuck to the adage, "Write what you know." I've been writing for years, and while I understand the truths of the writing life, how hard it is, how the competition is brutal, how it sometimes feels all the lights are being taken down on writing in so many ways, it's often hard to completely swallow these truths. My writer-narrators are disgruntled, hurt that they haven't made it the way actors, relegated to extra status, haven't made it, and they allow their discontent to hurt others, which is unforgivable. Rejection is a big part of a writer's life. Accepting rejection is also a big part. This push/pull of rejection/acceptance-of-failure is at the core of these two writing stories. And the narrator in each story receives enough pushback from the one he's strutting against, each a woman with her own problems, to recognize his discontent is minor compared to life's other discontents. People choose to be writers and to live a writing life. Writing is a self-imposed obstacle. For many, life doesn't provide choices. As Steve Almond wrote, the men in my stories are searching for a "better shake in things" and, along the way, recognize that Hollywood-style dreams and failures are often less daunting than the dreams and hardships of non-Hollywood life.

LC: "Usually when I write a book it takes three years from start to finish," you said in interview with *Sports Network*. In a later interview with writer Erika Dreifus, you mentioned that your third novel, *The Number of Missing*, took 12 years to write and revise. Apparently, the fourth book, *Both Members of the Club*, also spans years, beginning as a short story for an academic journal before being adapted into a novel, which became your graduate thesis. What's the backstory to your first two novels,

Headlock and *Belmondo Style*? Didn't *Belmondo Style* begin as short story for *Rain Dog Review*?

AB: *Headlock* was the fourth book-length manuscript I wrote and the first MS to get accepted. It was a great experience, getting that letter every budding novelist hopes for, and I had an excellent editor in Kathy Pories at Algonquin, who helped me shape the book. My grandfather was a wrestler in Russia, and I used that backstory to write a novel about the history of violence in a family. There's violence in one form or another in all my work, violence I try to write in a non-Hollywood way, and *Headlock* is a coming-of-age novel that shows a young man trying to control what's in his blood. *Belmondo Style* was my second novel, also a coming-of-age novel about a high school track star who comes out during the book. But *Belmondo Style* started as a story. The short story version is about a young man, new to NYC, living life as if he were Jean-Paul Belmondo. As you can see, I've had movie stars on my mind for a long time. He rubs his thumb across his lips like Belmondo in *Breathless*. He believes in only living for the moment. In the story, he picks up a married woman, spends the night with her, leaves in the morning, no-strings. His constant one-night stands are his movie moments, and he exits that story with a swagger. I liked the idea of a character trying to live like a movie and the connected truth that this lifestyle is impossible to sustain. I started writing a longer version of the story but quickly recognized the man's behavior would feel static. To dramatize the repercussions of his *Breathless*-lifestyle and to add conflict to the story, I knew I needed to come at the story from a different angle. So I gave the player a son, a kid who grew up feeling the effects of a father who's constantly moving from one woman to another. The son became the narrator. The father became a petty thief like Belmondo in *Breathless*. And I used a hate crime against the son to catalyze the plot and to show the beautiful bond between son and father, even when it played out against a violent backdrop.

LC: My understanding is that you had a notable literary agent, the late Robert Lescher, early on in your writing career. How did you come to work with him, and how influential was he in placing your first two novels with the big publishing houses Algonquin and St. Martin's Press?

AB: Robert Lescher was an old-school agent who gave me old-school attention. I was a kid writer when I contacted him, fresh out of grad school. I'd published a story in *Aethlon*, a respected journal of sports literature, and I sent that and a few other stories to him, and he took me on, which was very kind of him. Coincidentally, the day after I sold *Headlock* (I'd submitted the MS without an agent), Robert Lescher signed me. Bob negotiated the contract with Algonquin. And he sold *Belmondo Style* to St. Martin's. And he was trying to sell a version of *Both Members of the Club*, a short boxing novel, when he died. Having lunch with Bob at The Gramercy Tavern in NYC when we signed my first book contract was a day I felt like a real writer. My current agent is Alec Shane and he's been great, sticking by me even during lean years. He worked closely with me on a book that's out at publishers now, and I look up to him as an agent and an editor.

LC: What future projects are you working on? I read somewhere that you were focused on a further foray into boxing literature. Would that be a manuscript or a nonfiction work?

AB: With so many parallels between boxing and writing, especially the solitary work that goes into both, it's a great subject to write about and a great backdrop for novels and stories. I've written boxing fiction and a bunch of articles for boxing websites, but I'm probably done writing about the fights.

As for future projects, I've got a few things in the works. I have the novel out with my agent. I just finished a hybrid/flash prose piece I hope to place somewhere. And this summer, I'll do a final read-through of a novel I've been working on for a couple of years about race and art and the movement from apathy to engagement. The thematic threads in *All Around They're Taking Down the Lights* are in these projects. I think they're in almost all my published work—themes I must have been thinking about, at least subconsciously, before I started writing, when I moved to NYC at seventeen to study acting, dreaming Hollywood, but really dreaming, I think, of living a heightened life.

Thank you for these probing, insightful questions, Nicholas, and for your close reading of the stories in my collection (and some work outside my collection). I wish you consistently bright lighting at Lowestoft.

FORECLOSURE

Lee Clark Zumpe

That unoccupied domicile abides,
its once verdant lot much diminished
by ever-widening thoroughfares.

Withered flora settles in a neglected garden,
overzealous weeds constitute a jungle
that conceals the narrow sidewalk.

Within, perhaps hints of former lodgers –
absent so long neighbors cannot name them –
linger in secret recesses:

the spatter of stewing sauces,
the scent of aftershave,
the echoes of children's laughter.

And in the fusty shadows
of its moribund years,
tears, sweat, and anguish:

the hush of joyless holidays,
the tumult of escalating quarrels,
the desperation of eviction.

Slowly, vacancy takes a toll,
negligence undermines its foundations,
time and weather wear away its usefulness.

THE LIGUSTRUM NEEDS PRUNING

Lee Clark Zumpe

a mile from the gulf you can still smell
salt on the air some evenings
when the sea breeze
is just so.

here, on a strip of land that once had
more citrus trees than houses,
Sundays fade quickly
beneath doting live oaks.

the purple glow of evening
settles across the backyard,
gray barbeque smoke
curls in trees.

overgrown and full of deadwood,
the ligustrum needs pruning:
I wink and tell it
I'll catch it next weekend.

THE PIONEER HOTEL

Elizabeth Sowden

Sunday mornings in the Pioneer were the quietest. Sunlight filtered through the long, arched windows and made a geometric pattern that stretched across the scarred floorboards. A cord bearing a naked lightbulb snaked through the chicken-wire ceiling. George dressed in an ancient pair of Oxfords and a double-breasted suit. The suit was hopelessly out of style, but he'd found it for next to nothing at Nate's. His daughter, Millie, was meeting him for lunch one last time before she left town. George wanted to look nice.

In the pocket of the blazer, he found an old piece of penny candy. He knelt down by the foot of his aluminum bed and drummed his fingers against the wall. George twisted the cellophane wrapper and waited. Moments later, Bojack poked his head out of a crack in the wall, his tiny nose twitching. The rat flattened himself and squeezed out of the hole. He sat on his hind legs and put his little paws on George's hand. George stroked the rat's silky fur as it nibbled the candy.

George had named the rat after his two sons, Jack and Beau, both of whom he'd lost in the war. Jack was shot and then drowned in a shallow pool of seawater on Omaha Beach. And Beau...Beau wasn't technically dead. The Navy listed him as missing in action. A plane he was flying vanished somewhere off the coast of the Solomon Islands.

Someone in the next cage coughed. Bojack stiffened, then skittered back into his hole.

——— ✦ ———

Millie lit a cigarette as she waited outside the Pioneer Hotel. Hotel wasn't the right word for the place. Flop joint. Fleabox. Rat factory. Firetrap. Those were better words. She'd been inside once or twice; it stank of old men who didn't wash, backed-up toilets, and bean stew. The walls were stained brown from where the old geezers spit tobacco juice. Millie could have sworn that she had heard that the city planned to close down all of the cage hotels. Men boxed into closet-sized rooms and sleeping under chicken wire was unhealthy, they said.

Though Millie knew the city was probably right, she hoped they wouldn't shut down the Pioneer, or the Victor or the Beaufort. True, the flops were a far cry from the Palmer House, but where else could a man sleep for just a few cents per night? Her Pop's railroad pension paid him well, but he spent almost all of it on whiskey. Without the Pioneer, where would he go?

♦

George descended the staircase that led to the street. It was dark and steep, with only a small amount of light shining through the entryway below. He could see Millie through the glass.

"How are you, Pop?" Millie asked as George kissed her cheek. He gently tugged on one of her auburn curls and watched it snap back into place. With her fiery hair and plump cheeks, she looked just like her mother did when he first met her. She wore a white dress dotted with little strawberries and trimmed with red rickrack.

"That's some dress," he said. "I remember when I was a kid, your grandmother would never buy white fabric when she made clothes for us. She said it was too hard to keep clean. Back in the aughts, only ritzy people wore white."

"Maybe *I'm* ritzy," Millie sassed. She looped her arm through George's elbow. She was relieved he wasn't drunk. The men who lived in the Gateway District flops liked to start early.

"How much are they paying you this season?"

"Eighty dollars a week."

George whistled. "I worked for thirty-five years laying track for the Great Northern Railroad, and they never paid me even half that much."

They turned away from the Pioneer and walked south on Nicollet Avenue, past the liquor stores, the missions, the slop joints, and the other flops. George had stayed away from the

Persian Palms for three weeks to save up the money to take his daughter to a nice lunch before she went away for the entire summer. Avoiding the Palms had been tough, but he reminded himself that if he let a bunch of B-girls guzzle sloe gin on his dime, he wouldn't be able to buy his daughter anything nicer than a liverwurst sandwich and some boiled eggs. And Millie, she was a star, a star baseball player. She deserved better than slop, and he wasn't about to let *her* pay for it.

"I still have to get past the tryout," she said. In a few hours, Millie would board a train to Chicago, where she would report to Wrigley Field and fight for a spot in the All-American Girls Professional Baseball League.

"You've got past the tryout every year for the past ten years! What are you worried about?"

"My shoulder aches a bit. My pitching arm. Ever since they switched us to pitching overhand, like the men in the Majors do, my shoulder's been aching. It's not bad. Well, not *real* bad. I can still pitch. It's fine."

"You're darn right it's fine! You remember when I hurt my knee all those years ago? Lugging railroad ties in the mud. I slipped and twisted my knee. Felt like the whole thing was just shredded. But I still worked. I still worked until it was time to retire, and they gave me my pension."

Millie remembered. Two of the men he worked with carried him up the stairs to their house. He was drunk from the whiskey they'd given him. He tried to kiss her, and she recoiled from the smell. The next morning, he went to work. He never missed work, and his knee never healed.

———— ✦ ————

The oak-paneled dining room at Charlie's Cafe Exceptionale was lit softly with candles. George and Millie sipped Presidents — a cocktail made with gin, grenadine, orange, and lemon juice. George ordered the steak in butter sauce, while Millie opted for the *pompano en papillote*: fish fillets in a buttery mushroom and seafood sauce, baked in parchment paper.

"I oughta come see one of your games this year," George said.

He stabbed a piece of steak with his fork. "I could save up my money. Buy a train ticket."

Millie picked up her glass and breathed in the piney scent of the gin. "That would be great, Pop."

She pictured her father in the stands at the ballpark in Rockford or Racine. She took a long sip of her drink.

For dessert, they shared a flaming Cherries Jubilee. The waiter doused the blood-red cherries with brandy and struck a match. Blue flames erupted and quickly burned away.

———— ✦ ————

The clock tower on top of the train depot cast a long shadow over the street. Millie retrieved her small suitcase from temporary storage. George walked her to the platform.

"See you in September, Pop," she said. He put his arms around her. She could smell the flophouse in the fabric of his suit: sweat, stew, and tobacco.

"Write to me when you can," he said.

Millie felt her throat tighten. She stepped onto the train and glanced through the train window at her father, who was still standing on the platform.

George waited until the train pulled out of the station and then headed straight for the Persian Palms.

———— ✦ ————

On the train, Millie tried to sleep, but the compartment was too warm. After Pop's knee injury, he started drinking more. Sometimes, he'd stay in a flophouse in the Gateway District and sleep it off if he'd had too many. When he brought lice into the house after returning from a flop, Mom said the next time he went to one of those flea pits, he should just stay there.

A week later, Pop moved into the Pioneer Hotel and never came home again. Even though the Pioneer was just two miles away from their house, Millie didn't see Pop for years.

Then the war happened. At Jack's funeral, Millie sat in the front row, staring down at her shoes. The old wooden pew groaned as someone sat next to her. She felt a gentle arm around her shoulders and smelled whiskey. Millie rested her head on

Pop's shoulder and felt his whiskers against her forehead. Beau, who was on leave for the funeral, sat on the other side of Pop, who wound his free arm around his living son. Beau wore his dress blues and Millie a new skirt suit made of black tweed. Pop's old three-piece pinstripe suit still looked dapper; you had to look closely to see the threadbare edges on the lapels.

Through the train window, Millie could see that the sky was turning from black to purple. She would arrive in Chicago soon. She needed to sleep. She squeezed her eyes shut and felt a tear roll down the side of her nose.

———— ✦ ————

George spent the last of his cash on whiskey sours at the Persian Palms. His friend Cornelius slung an arm around George's back and helped him climb the stairs at the Pioneer.

"My wife went to Montana," George slurred as he plopped onto his bed. "Sh' sol' the house 'n married someone else."

"I know," Cornelius nodded drowsily. He was drunk too.

"An' my girl's gone. Gone 'til Sept…September."

"I know."

"An' my boys…" Tears dampened George's grizzled cheeks.

"Sleep. Sleep. We gotta sleep," said Cornelius as he helped George take off his shoes. George closed his eyes.

A few hours later, after the effects of the whiskey had worn off, George lay awake, listening to the sounds of men snoring. He heard a scratching sound and reached an arm over the side of the bed, his knuckles brushing against the floor. Bojack's eyes glowed like embers in the dark. The rat crept silently over the dusty floorboards and sniffed George's fingers. George scooped the rat up and placed the animal on his chest. He folded both hands over the rat's back and tickled its soft belly with his thumbs. The rat nuzzled George's chin.

———— ✦ ————

The tender grass at Wrigley Field shimmered under the afternoon sun. Millie gripped the ball with her thumb and two fingers. She brought her knee up to her chest and kicked, twisting her body and releasing the ball. She watched it break just as it crossed the plate. The batter swung and missed.

Two managers stood near the on-deck circle watching Millie pitch. She knew them both; she'd played under them, on different teams. One of them clenched a cigar end between his teeth. Two seasons ago, in a one-run game, he yanked Millie from the mound when a left-handed batter came up to the plate. The pitcher who took over gave up a home run on the first pitch, costing them the game. She stared at him now with narrowed eyes.

The catcher tossed the ball back to Millie, who held her glove up to her face as she switched to a changeup grip. Her changeup would seal the deal. It always did. She set up for the pitch, and as she released the ball, she felt it roll off her fingertips. The batter hacked at air. Sweat trickled down the back of Millie's neck. She heard nothing other than the sound of the ball smacking the leather of the catcher's mitt.

In the shower after the tryout, Millie felt a pinch in her shoulder. *It's fine*, she told herself. So long as it didn't bother her while she was on the mound, she could live with it.

Maybe after the season was over, she'd have enough money to buy a house for her and Pop so he could finally stop living in a cage.

———— ✦ ————

In the day room at the Pioneer, George played cards with Cornelius and two other guys. On a small television, black-and-white footage of Mickey Mantle talking to a reporter played without sound. George wished that they would show Millie's baseball games on TV. Ten years in the league, and he had never once seen her play.

"I should save up my money and buy a train ticket," George said to no one in particular. "I should go see my Millie play ball. Both of my boys played in high school. I never made it to their games." After all, Millie might not have many more seasons of play left in her. She had said so herself; her shoulder bothered her. George had pretended not to be concerned because he didn't want her to get in her head about it. But he knew if she injured it, it could change everything for her.

"Whatcha got there, Mack?" Cornelius asked. George turned and saw Mack standing behind them. He was a tall, broad-shouldered man who wore his shirt open at the collar, revealing a gold saint's medal on a knotted chain. He held the limp body of a dead rat in one of his large hands.

"Do you believe this?" Mack asked, holding up the rat for the men to see. Mack was the owner of the Pioneer. He also owned the liquor store next door and a bar around the corner. "It's huge. If I didn't know better, I'd think one of you degenerates was feedin' him."

George looked closely at the rat. Its eyes were squeezed shut, and its mouth was open, its tongue faintly stained with something green. George bit the inside of his lip to keep from crying.

———— ✦ ————

At dusk, Washington Avenue was dark except for the glowing marquee lights of the Persian Palms. George felt the sky above him spinning as he sat on the sidewalk, blood dripping from his face onto the pavement. The neon signs in the windows cast a red glare over everything. In the light, his blood looked black. It was sticky.

Out of the corner of his eye, George saw a policeman standing on the other side of the street. George struggled to get to his feet and walk in the opposite direction. He couldn't take another night in the drunk tank.

———— ✦ ————

A few days later, the purple bloom underneath George's eye started to fade. He drummed his fingers against the wall and waited, even though he knew Bojack would not appear. Cashless, he sat through a preacher's sermon on temperance at the Union City Mission in exchange for a root beer and a hot beef sandwich. After leaving the mission, he joined his friends in Gateway Park. They shared a bottle of wine.

Back at the Pioneer, Mack was standing behind the desk in the lobby.

"George," Mack said, "this came for you."

Mack handed him a postcard that showed a picture of a boat

in a blue harbor. On the back, Millie had written her new address in South Bend.

"Pitching for South Bend Blue Sox," she wrote. "Team looks good this year. First game in Kenosha. Write soon."

At the very bottom, where there was hardly any space to write, Millie printed in tiny letters, "See you in September."

VOLTA

Diana Senechal

When we were young, we fancied ourselves grey, Adam the world-weary dreamer, I the worker. We met at Ashley's, where we both scooped ice cream earnestly one summer. He had flunked an English class at Yale (he could have gotten an A if he had just done the reading) and was attending summer school for a remedial credit; I was laboring my way through a communication major at the University of New Haven, scraping together any jobs I could find, seizing every scrap of free time for study, and hosting a music show once a week at WNHU. I paid my own tuition with loans and a scholarship. Flunking a class was not in the picture. But Adam intrigued me with his floppy, lackadaisical ways.

He was schooled and versed in suffering: the late-night news crossed his lips at the start of each shift. "Did you hear about El Salvador?" he asked once. A bit of a language geek, I nimbly pointed out the difference between "Have you heard of" and "Did you hear about," trying to shift the topic. But no, he wasn't having it. There had been another massacre by army troops. "Yes, but what about your homework?" I asked. He glumly told me that he was supposed to write a sonnet but couldn't get his mind off the news—or drunken roommates banging out the blues.

He lived with three musicians, Pablo, Jon, and Geoff (he had just moved off campus and planned to stay off). He thought blues musicians would teach him something about form, at least through their vibrations, but they proved a ragtag bunch, given to long, wayward jams and hapless vocals ("I love my baby, it's so hard to see her with you, Jim"). He sometimes escaped to the local café for relative quiet, only to be accosted along the way by homeless beggars or curbside preachers pressing us to pray, all of us, the whole sinful earth. He didn't take the proselytizing personally; he saw himself as a mere sprat in their teeming school. Still, it broke his concentration once again. "You've got to move out and find a quieter place," I told him. He knew, he knew. Then I offered to let him move in with me (I had an extra room; my roommate had moved out). To my surprise, he arrived with his boxes and bags the following week.

That gave our friendship a boost but also knocked me temporarily off course. With the money saved from rent, I figured I could splurge a little. We took the Metro North train about once a week to New York. At oyster bars, we slurped our cash away. The waiters took a liking to us; they knew our names, and we their shells and brews. After a couple dozen, we headed onward to our favorite pubs. We talked late into the night: I about old-time radio, and he about poems he was trying to write. I nagged him until he actually wrote them (the sonnet was the only one he never wrote). Somehow, we made it through the summer and later through college. We never dated—this was all platonic—but one autumn night in our senior year, we lay side by side on my bed. "Are we supposed to be together?" I asked. No answer came. The question hung like a pair of pants that have slipped to one end of a hanger.

Then, years went by, and we began to use our learnings at last. He, I read on the newly arisen Internet, had become the editor-in-chief of a renowned literary journal; I had gone into cable TV production and been promoted several times. My salary probably quadrupled his, but he had ten times the prestige. I only had to mention his name in certain circles, and eyes would pop out. "You actually *know* Adam Wilt?"

I met Scott, another producer, who became my beloved husband. Even with our hefty salaries, we thought domestically and lived frugally, dining on broccoli and rice in the kitchen, giving up all things gourmet (with slips here and there). We eschewed shop talk; our daily conversation had to do with the toilet handle that needed replacing, the cracked tile in the hallway, and the results of my latest pregnancy test. When our first child, Marcella, popped out into the world, we embraced home even more fervently, telecommuting whenever we could, until our twin boys arrived and I took a hiatus from work, the first hiatus of my life. From here, Scott started spending more time at the studio, where his duties had increased. For my part, I started indulging in daydreaming. My days had bursts and snatches of rush, but usually, in the late morning, when Kyle and Kurt were napping, I set the coffee brewing and sat by the window, gazing out at the magnolia tree and wondering what had become of Adam besides his career.

One day, I received a handwritten letter from him, already an oddity in our times. We have given up penmanship and postage for sheer speed, and I understand why. The miracle of tapping out a message and hearing back within minutes! The emphasis on *content*, for Christ's sake, not curlicues! Granted, I was curious enough about the content of this letter, handwritten though it might be. "Dear Charlotte," he wrote, "We live a sobered life." (*Who is this "we"? A royal "we"? Or has he found a partner? Or is he speaking of the two of us or of the human condition?*) I read on. "We do our duty, then seek out repose. But if you think we've wisened, look at how the wars rage on, now with new technologies. How did September 11 happen? How could intelligence be so obtuse? Our folly frolics forth, now in reverse." (*Save that line!* I told him in my mind. *Oh, yes, and I figured out the "we," it's humanity you're talking about, as usual.*)

I started to pen a reply. My hand was clumsy now; I had to restart several times. I told him of my life as a mother of three: of diapers, walks to the nearby park, and the books I read them at night. I also told him (a little more shyly) about my trips to the gym, my sea salt soaks, my high-fiber vegetarian diet. Creaking and grey, we boast of bursting youth; it's a badge of honor, at forty-two, to be told you look no older than twenty-five, though there must come a point when the sincerity of such a statement becomes strained.

One of the secret reasons for my hiatus was to regain my youthful figure. This had worked: I had shed twenty pounds, returned to calisthenics, and started rediscovering the alluring dresses from my college days. They say age is in the mind; in this, you'll find an admixture of truth. I had passed forty but felt fresh and sharp. Burdens had lifted even as duties had accrued. Yes, I cared about my appearance, but once I hit a certain standard, I stopped worrying about it and stopped worrying in general. Life seemed plentiful and good. "Friends say we have a perk to us, a glow," I wrote, using the plural to stress my married state. It wasn't a lie, either; Scott might not have had Adam's dreamy manner, but he was well-toned, fiery-eyed, brutally funny. Together, we had the verve of high school sweethearts.

I ended the letter, rummaged for an envelope, found it, came upon a stamp in the corner of my drawer, and put the completed act in my bag with the intent of mailing it on our way to the park. Plurals had taken over my life; I had concrete reasons, besides marriage, for the "we." But sometimes, such as now, the "I" stuck out in my soul despite my wording. An unfamiliar melancholy rose up in my neck. I wondered why Adam had written. Did he miss me? Did he want to let me know how he was? He hadn't even told me; his letter seemed more protest than disclosure. Railing on about calamity had always been his way of saying hi. Then it hit me that I might never see him again—not because I couldn't, not because our paths had no chance of crossing, but simply because years go by, and eventually, something or other will take him or me out of the world. We think we still have time for everything, but young or old, we lurch toward the hearse.

I pulled the slightly crumpled envelope (scrunched beneath my wallet) out of my bag. I had forgotten to mail it; we were at the park, Kyle and Kurt playing in the sandbox, filling and emptying their buckets with glee. I tore it open, pulled out the letter, and unfolded it on my thigh. "P.S.," I wrote in shaky print (cursive had always eluded me). "Remember that sonnet you never wrote? Here you go. Cheers." I wrote it out.

> When we were young, we fancied ourselves grey
> and versed in suffering: the late-night news,
> or drunken roommates banging out the blues,
> or curbside preachers pressing us to pray.
> At oyster bars, we slurped our cash away;
> they knew our names, and we their shells and brews,
> then, years went by, and we began to use
> the kitchen, giving up all things gourmet.
> But if you think we've wisened, look at how
> our folly frolics forth, now in reverse:
> creaking and grey, we boast of bursting youth.
> In this, you'll find an admixture of truth—
> friends say we have a perk to us, a glow—
> but young or old, we lurch toward the hearse.

Then I realized I couldn't mail it. It would enable and confine him in bad ways. My therapist and I had been discussing how, if you do too much for others, you take away their agency. The sonnet was Adam's, not mine; I hadn't even known until now that I could write one. It wasn't half bad: silly at moments ("lurch toward the hearse"?), but definitely a sonnet. Adam should have written it; given that he hadn't, I had to let it go.

Or so I thought for years. Looking back now, I see that I had twisted a basic wisdom. Yes, one should avoid doing unto others what they need to do unto themselves, but that wasn't an issue here. The homework assignment had long faded; sending Adam a sonnet wouldn't have taken away an iota of his agency, which now towered far above remedial credits. Besides, it would have been nice to answer him; we might have stayed in touch here and there. Oh, the babble we come up with, the excuses we concoct just to avoid those almost-friends, the people at the edges of our minds.

THE COMPLETE POEMS OF JOHN KEATS
William Miller

The shipping cost more than the book
with all the poems, less and great,
the odes and their veiled goddesses,
sorrow glutted on a morning rose.

Inside the front cover was a handwritten note—
a woman planned to meet a man
for the first time, directions to the off-ramp,
the coffee shop spelled out in a careful hand.

Did they meet? Did they fall in love?
Was she crushed by a first impression,
how he talked while eating his scone?
Did she see the scar above his eye,

were his eyes deep blue, piercing
the last wall she'd built around
herself, the room where she hid
with her favorite poems, a potted plant?

I see them at the table, sitting with two
double lattes, hopeful with all the hope
a first date allows, frozen like figures
on an urn, forever young.

"LADY MACBETH"

William Miller

Once a month, sometimes three nights a week,
she came out to the courtyard
in her pink, taffeta nightgown
with the torn hem, a bottle of discount wine
in her hand.

We watched, waited for the performance
to begin. On the best nights, the moon,
waxing or waning, lit the flagstones
like a spotlight, turned her face
whiter than pale.

Her broken monologue always came back
to a married man who left his wife for her,
a son who "od'd" and blamed them both
for "the needle tracks" in his arms.

She spun with the bottle, an awkward dance,
sang snatches of a sixty's folk song
about hippies with flowers
in their hair.... Our sins seemed small,
little things next to her ritual guilt,

as we looked down from our narrow windows,
green shutters we bolted with an iron hook
after she went back inside,
laughing, crying, blaming
only herself.

LOVE MORE

Barbara Bottner

She was no cheater. She was a faithful person. That's who she knew herself to be. At least since college, anyway. She had to stick close to her integrity so she could respect herself. She was firm about this, at least when she wasn't half-naked in a hotel suite with Peter, her long-lost housemate from Paris. She knew the problems with her husband, Dan, would have to be faced head-on. Concretely. Like a grown-up. Not some teenager whose wild libido was running the show.

Why was her marriage so conflicted? She considered this while she drank her coffee. It went back, inevitably, to her father. Or, more precisely, her father issues. No woman growing up with Seymour would have emerged without some significant warping of body and soul. Or could she lay the problem at her late mother's feet? A psychic once told her that the two lineages that created her should have never come together, so there was that.

At about eleven AM, she was ready to face her life. She decided new doors don't open as long as you carry old baggage. So, the first order was to deal with Lili's ashes, which had ridden around in the trunk of her car for months, waiting for the right spot in which to spend eternity. She went to her car, retrieved the urn, and carried it into the backyard. Deal with this, girlfriend, she whispered to herself, but before long, her motivation leaked away. No matter what form Lili was in, she had the effect of making Stormy feel deficient and at a loss. Lili was powerful dead or alive.

Actually, if Stormy was being honest, she wasn't ready. In fact, she deserved a break. She set the urn down in a flower bed and, smack in the middle of the day, went inside. She poured herself a large glass of a Cabernet. Or a Merlot. Whichever. She didn't really like wine and couldn't tell them apart. She headed to her luxurious velvet couch. To the outside eye, it would look as if she was goofing off. Maybe she was. Writers could never be sure when they were working.

A Manhattanite in exodus, she thumbed through the most recent issue of *The New Yorker*. A Joyce Carol Oates piece captured her attention. She'd always felt better when she read essays penned by brilliant women who were unattractive in high school.

It was a long essay, and she became slightly drowsy. She stretched, preparing perhaps, for a short nap. Why not? But aggressive pounding on the front door brought her back. She was not inclined to be disturbed and ignored it. The Cab slid down her throat, so comforting. The pounding continued. It took an effort for her to kick back and be useless.

"Answer, goddamned it! It's your father!" barked Seymour through a window. There was an unusual urgency in his voice. "He wants to talk to you!"

The massive front door swung wide open. Right. Seymour had her house key, a fact she was forced to reckon with as he stood in front of her proudly, perfumed and spiffy. He was wearing his golf cap, golf shorts, and matching Pima cotton shirt, perfectly tailored and meticulously ironed. This stout melody in lilac confronted her as determined as an agent from the IRS. Only he wasn't wearing IRS-black; even his socks, which covered his knock knees, were lavender. He was also sporting gardener's gloves which, in turn, were holding an unlikely accessory for him, a shovel. His green eyes seemed as bright as a traffic light, a traffic light that was now attempting to hypnotize her by standing directly over her and glowering.

"I haven't been over here for a long time," he said as if she used to invite him for high tea with some regularity. They hadn't seen each other since that dreadful fight at his country club. She was not remotely in the mood.

"Hello," she said flatly.

"How about a little more enthusiasm?"

"Okay. Top of the morning to you!" She sat up slightly, but she still stayed enmeshed in the big down pillows, one of which she held in front of her.

He pointed to the shovel and nodded with importance.

"The gardener was here yesterday, dad."

"Sharon, your father is suffering. He came to help you." Seymour pointed to the backyard as if she could follow his logic.

"I'm not up for help," she said. "I'm trying to be lazy."

"Well, be lazy another day," he commanded and ambled into the kitchen, humming. He poured himself a glass of water. He could hum and suffer simultaneously. She grabbed her wine and gulped it.

He had such an assured air about him. As a kid, she hung on to his every word. Back then, she wanted to make him proud of her. Thus, she practiced millions of pirouettes, mastered a decent French accent, learned to argue politics and how to pitch a speedy softball, and shoot a decent basketball. For her father, all, everything, anything she could do, she did for him; he had been her one hope.

The same instinct still sat inside her; she could feel it trembling in her gut. That was why, she supposed, when she deciphered his mission to help her bury Lili's urn, she reluctantly stood up.

"What happened? Did your golf game get canceled?"

"Don't be a smart ass." So, that was a 'yes.'

"And you honestly came here to help me do this?"

"I feel terrible. I want to be closer to you," he said, his eyes blazing like a verdant meadow after a rain. He glared with a 'what are you waiting for?' look, the one he used so effectively to intimidate his staff. She shrugged. This was an insane intrusion, yet she headed outside to the flower bed and picked up the urn. Seymour followed her. He leaned on his shovel, an unlikely eighty-five-year-old Jewish suburban still-life.

"Where do you want it?"

Good question. She looked around for where she thought Lili

belonged. Boomer, her dear old Lab retriever, was buried almost at the property line on the east corner. Did she want her pet to have to deal with her mother? Boomer, who got love right. She walked over to his spot.

"I miss you, pooch," she mumbled, and her chest tightened with sorrow.

Seymour stepped closer. *"What?"*

How could she explain doggie love?

Seymour turned his head, taking in the perimeter of the place, mumbling to himself. Then, without any instruction from her whatsoever, his shovel hit the grass just beyond the pool and smack in the middle of their half-acre.

"*No,* dad! That's where we open our lounge chairs, exactly right there!"

"Lounge there!" he pointed west. "This, here, *this* is the spot." Her father had been a CEO of a large company. After decades of commanding people and watching them hop to it, he'd forgotten how to speak to regular humans. He was used to them apologizing, even when it should have been the other way around. He pulled that on her, too, when she was a kid. Yet people liked him. Various secretaries insisted they did when Stormy occasionally went to lunch with them. "Your father…" they'd say, "he's tough." Then they'd grin with genuine affection. But who knew what their story really was? He was their boss, after all. And he was sleeping with half of them.

"Can't! Because if we have to move our chairs, we'll get too much sun," she explained.

"Buy an umbrella, and you'll have plenty of shade."

"That's *not* where I want it!" she said petulantly. She was six, and he'd taken away her ice cream.

"The trouble with you is there is never the perfect spot." He started digging for real.

"What are you saying? Spit it out."

"I don't get why it's so hard for you to let go of that woman."

He knew why. But he was a coward. She wished she could take the shovel and clock him for being so dense. Anyway, he was too old for this. But he was at it. Dirt was flying all over. Nothing wrong with his testosterone. He was muttering Yiddish phrases under his breath.

Then, a clang. "Whaddya got here, a damn boulder?"

"It's probably a *rock,* dad. Not every piece of land in the world is as smooth as your clubhouse lawn. Nor is life itself. Life has boulders!"

"Spare me the sociology lesson. If only you would have learned to play golf, maybe things would have been different between us. I offered. Private lessons! You could've started anytime."

He was sweating under his arms, a swath of dampness across his back. The young Seymour was suddenly there, a guy going after what he wanted; defiant, strong, physical, not the club dandy with too much time on his hands and too much libido for an old guy.

"I would help, but I'm tipsy," she explained. "I drank a fair amount of wine. I got tired of thinking about my life."

"And those are your choices?!" He bent over, all rickety five foot nine inches of him, and picked up the urn. His legs wobbled, and his barrel chest suddenly seemed unsteady. The urn was not that heavy, but still, he staggered. She worried that he would lose his balance, but he shoved it over the spot he'd dug. She thought: *you're* a pisser, you old fart.

He heaved a huge mound of earth to the side. "I think this is deep enough," he panted. "Nope, too shallow."

He picked up the urn and threw himself at the task again, but his cream-colored shoe got caught in the pile of dirt. He tried to shake it loose, and this time, he lost his balance completely. He went for his shovel, which fell, and then, as if it was happening in slow motion, down he went, the lavender melody crashing onto the moist dirt.

He was yelling, "Oy, oy vey. Oy vey ish mere."

His arm reached under him, touching his lumbar region. This is where they, of rigid Austrian heritage, lock in their emotions.

"Dad, dad, dad! Are you okay? Dad, say something. You have your breath? Any pain? *Dad!*"

"Stop screaming! I'm fine. *Fine.* This is how it is to be an old man," he protested, then looked at her as if this was an unfair fact and she should do something about it.

She circled him with her arms. He'd always been an athlete, but today she could feel only how light he was, like a child of ten or eleven. She was careful; even a hairline fracture in an octogenarian was serious. She decided to try to get him up into one of the garden chairs, which, though cushion-less, was right nearby.

'Ouch!" he said resentfully. He was a staunch member of the club that believed fury was always helpful.

"Ouch, *what?* Where?"

"Dizzy," maybe.

"Dizzy would be a concussion. Did you fall on your head? No, you didn't. You're not dizzy."

"Maybe a little disoriented." He wrestled away from her.

"Nope, dad, we're going inside." He didn't protest as she helped him step up into the house.

"I didn't finish the job," he objected. "And you, you'll *never* do it without me!" Her father never entertained incompetence, which is why he wouldn't allow himself to hear what she had to say to him. Failure wasn't an option. Yet sometimes, she thought she saw a slice of worry cross his face as if there was an inner knowing, but then he'd change the subject or make a joke.

"You're in shock. Don't talk." Stormy almost threw him on the couch. She felt his racing pulse. She brought him a glass of water, untied his shoes, and took them off.

"What are you doing?" he gripped his toes.

"Making you comfortable." He acted as if he was giving in to some radical untested therapy; shoe removal.

"Thank God you won't be able to cart me around in the trunk of your car when I go; I wouldn't like that. I have a plot. You could be next to me if you weren't so obstinate."

"But I am." Stormy put a pillow under his knees.

"You're goddamned right, you are. If you'd done this when she died, I could be on the ninth hole; look what a gorgeous day it is."

"I didn't ask you to come here. In fact, I was having a nice afternoon alone with my *New Yorker*."

"Wasting your life."

She sighed. It was hopeless. "You know what? As soon as you feel a little better, I'd like you to leave."

He laughed. "I should care what you think!"

Her father liked arguments. They served a purpose, to ensure him of his power. To reduce life to black and white. To make him believe he could beat death, or something like that.

He wiped his forehead with his lilac handkerchief.

She felt her heart about to pound with fury. "Let's not fight. Just rest up."

He laughed again. "You're bossing *me* around? It's funny, you know that?"

"Oh, right, you're the only boss in the room."

"I'm the only one who ran a five-million-dollar company with forty people under him and made fourth-quarter profits Wall Street couldn't believe."

"Your favorite subject---tra la tra la. Money!"

"I'm leaving you plenty of it one day."

"Again, I didn't ask you for it. And I don't want it."

He worked to sit back up; Machiavelli would never suggest fighting half-prone. "*You don't want it?* Give me the phone. I'll call my lawyer right now!"

"Marvin Kopelman, right? How is old Marvin? What's his number? I'll dial."

Seymour half rose off the couch, stumbled, and grabbed the

phone from her hands. "You..you…"

"Me, what? I'm such a big bother? I haven't asked you for anything since my last year of college when you decided not to pay my tuition."

His sallow complexion was turning into an agitated rosy glow now. "You disobeyed me."

"Right. You disapproved of my boyfriend. So, you kept me from graduating?"

"I wanted a better life for you." He collapsed back on the sofa.

"A better life? As in becoming a waitress and taking two more years to graduate. If I forgot to thank you, let me take the opportunity now!"

"You didn't respect yourself," he mumbled undaunted. "I didn't want that for you."

She had been desperate for love, but until this moment, she didn't realize he'd ever noticed.

"Dad…" she said in a lower octave, "I was lost."

"And that's *my* fault?"

"I didn't say that."

"But it's what you think."

Bingo.

"*Ouch*!" he gripped his side fiercely.

"What? Why are you screaming?"

"A pain in my side!"

"I'll call your doctor." She ran to get the phone.

Peels of laughter. "You love me, see? You don't want me to die." He released his hand. "No pain. I'm fine." He smiled benignly.

"*Jesus,* Seymour!"

Her dad had wrestled in college. Now he was wrestling again with her.

"I'm sorry. I don't know what gets into me sometimes, Sharon. Maybe I'm afraid of dying."

That shut her up.

"Let's have something to drink," he said, suddenly convivial;

the afternoon clearly wasn't over for him. "A nice glass of wine for your dad?" He patted the couch.

"No. I'm not your friend. "

"I'll tell you what I *do* feel a little badly about, Sharon."

So, he was going to apologize after all! She tried to quiet herself down.

"I never took you on the Concord when it was flying." His green eyes were glued to her brown ones. "I feel awful about that."

Well, he had to begin somewhere. "Got it," she said magnanimously. True, for years, she hoped he'd invite her along. "Hey, Stormy, let me show you Paris on the company's dollar."

"Forgiven. Anything else you want to say?"

"There's nothing else. From where I came from, I did good."

It was their personal half-time, and they stared at each other.

"Why didn't I think to invite you on one of those jaunts?" He slipped into reverie: "The service was amazing. The food was Continental, and the seats were tipped back so that after you ate, you could snooze, and then, bingo, you were in New York City, ready for the day. I *did* bring you back some nice pearl earrings from one of my trips."

She had those earrings somewhere. She wore them with mixed feelings. A present, yes, but she would have loved to have picked them out herself on The Champs Elysees.

"I've never flown first class." She couldn't help the tightness in her lips.

His face blanched in pain. *"Never?"*

"Never, ever."

"That's my fault, too, I suppose?"

"It doesn't matter."

"I'm glad you're not a total nut case. But you still insist on believing Lili was Jack the Ripper. Why do you hang on to that story?"

He was galaxies away from her now, and no words came, none at all.

"So, you forgive me about the Concord?"

So, Seymour was not going to look back on his life. He was too insecure. This fact startled her; he was too weak, not too strong.

She closed her eyes and tried to remember a Buddhist sutra. It was that or tears. She muttered in Sanskrit under her breath.

"Your father feels better now. You don't realize it, but he is an emotional man." Now Seymour's face relaxed. His eyes blinked. He'd stopped hiding.

She got up to get him a glass of water. When she returned, his eyes were closed again.

"I wasn't that great a father," he mumbled. "Too busy." He opened his eyes again. "But I wasn't that bad, either."

He sipped slowly, thoughtfully. Then, he was up, shuffling towards the front door.

"Very emotional afternoon," he announced, his forehead slightly shiny and his outfit creased. "But *good!*"

Stormy took stock of his disappearing corpus. He famously chased women but chose to run from the very one who was born adoring him. He kept walking. On his slightly bowlegs, he made it outside and headed to his car, mumbling, "good! *Not* bad!"

And then, the smooth rumble of his motor as he backed out of her driveway, a deafeningly loud instrumental blasting from his radio. It was as if a typhoon had come and gone, and the place was leveled, leaving the afternoon strangely empty.

Stormy returned to the couch to finish the *New Yorker* article, then brought the wine glass to the sink and wandered into her bedroom. She dug out the pearl earrings her father had bought her years ago. She put them on in front of the mirror. They framed her face perfectly.

She had to admit, they looked wonderful. They really did.

ESPÈCE DE COWBOY

Charles Holdefer

I first met Lise back in the U.S. during my student days at one of those wonderful American institutions that you might as well call Pizza U. (You chose your major the way you chose toppings. You paid your money, you got your degree.) I'd chosen business administration. In those days, my world wasn't too complicated. My main interests were earning money and having a girlfriend. Since I'd always been pretty good at math, business seemed the best route for my future. Engineering would've been too much work; plus, the male-to-female ratio in engineering was unacceptable. At the Pizza U Business School, in addition to girls (*hundreds* of them, tweezering their legs in the lecture hall, squeezing their books against their chests: never had learning been so exciting!), I discovered that there were also plenty of lost and confused people. This had the effect of making me look good: a guy who knew what he was about.

Promising, as the letters of recommendation like to say. And the finest part of all was meeting my fiancée.

Lise had studied political science at the most elite graduate school in Paris. Now she was in the U.S. getting a one-year MBA, which was fashionable then for a certain slice of the French elite, another notch on their CVs. How she ended up at Pizza U was a mystery to me: some kind of administrative shipwreck, I suppose. We met at a Halloween party, and instantly I was attracted. Not because she was foreign and sophisticated and from a tony school. I knew none of that, then. And when one of her first remarks was to explain for my edification that Halloween wasn't really American, but rather a manifestation of a Celtic rite, which we Americans had appropriated for our consumer society, I was hardly listening. I was looking at her, not simply ogling but also wondering what her costume was supposed to be. It certainly wasn't obvious. (I clutched a black hood in my hand because it was too hot and itchy to wear; being an executioner was less fun than I'd imagined.) Lise wore the same shade of robin's egg blue, from her pumps to her satin skirt to the scarf around her neck; her lipstick, too, was an airy blue that in the presence of so many macabre costumes set her apart. There was something about the way she carried herself, excessively formal for a Halloween Party. I almost told her this but kept my mouth shut.

What she saw in me is harder to say. Lise was out of her element, that was for sure, and in such circumstances, people can get lonely and behave differently than they might otherwise. Seductions can happen, like falling downstairs. Also, it turns out she didn't think I was bad looking, in a lean cowboy sort of way. Not long after that first party (this sounds silly, but the truth often is), Lise dressed me up with a hat and jeans and a little leather vest and then surveyed the result, which seemed to affect her strongly: she kept touching me and laughing.

"My, Wally!" she said and laughed.

"That's me," I said.

This was a new experience. She would touch my shoulders, tug my belt, then laugh some more. I didn't feel insulted because it was light-hearted and friendly and because when she walked a circle, touching and laughing, her laughter seemed to include herself, too, the whole of humanity, all our follies. It made me laugh with her. Then she kissed me on the mouth.

Clearly, this was a game that appealed to her. I tapped the brim of my hat and promised I'd give her America, all of it, and she grinned and continued to touch, more boldly now.

And when I think back on those days and on our engagement, a time when, in the usual childish manner of people in love, the question of how we might appear to the rest of the world was either a matter of indifference or a source of foolish pride, the main thing that I recall is our belief. Our belief in *us*.

Paris didn't love me. Besides, we discovered, upon our arrival, that Lise's father was dying. So, from the outset, there were far more important things to worry about than welcoming the New Boy in Town. Lise was devastated; she and her mother spent their time going back and forth to the Hôpital Saint-Joseph. I accompanied them occasionally, but it was not really my place. During this grim interval, I often found myself alone in their rue Gay-Lussac apartment, a dim two-bedroom above a Hungarian travel agency. I spent my time watching a TV that I couldn't understand (except the weather reports—all those maps and symbols) and, from my second day, snooping around the premises. Prying became my chief source of entertainment. I pawed through Lise's childhood and adolescent effects, familiarizing myself, getting to know her better, and in another room discovered—oops!— some pornographic magazines that must've belonged to Papa, the same unlucky Papa who now lay agonizing on a hospital bed. (The guy definitely had a thing for Asian women, tropical settings. I wondered if his wife knew.) In the beginning, I didn't go out much because it seemed inappropriate to play the fun-loving tourist while the rest of the household spent the day with hospital horrors. Each evening Lise and her mother came home tearful and distraught. The Official Fiction was that Walter kept busy all day studying his French grammar lessons, in view of his smooth integration and general self-improvement, but in truth, I mainly mooned around and daydreamed. In those early days, without Lise's excellent English as my crutch, communication would've been impossible. Lise's mother spoke French to me in long gusts; at times, I could feel my hair blowback, but I could muster little in reply. Clearly, I wasn't a natural when it came to languages. I remember squinting out the apartment windows at passersby in the street below, women in boots, scooter boys with cropped heads and retro-helmets, a lanky man in a striped djellaba, clasping prayer beads, and it struck me that even the manner of walking was not the same as in America; when people hailed each other, the language of their arms was different, too.

But I wasn't completely alone in the apartment: Clo-Clo, the family terrier, accompanied me with clicking toenails as I went from room to room, watching my every move, sniffing in drawers as I opened them. I fed him chocolate-covered cherries till he threw up; he had his share of the fun, too. I talked to Clo-Clo in English, and his liquid brown eyes expressed a degree of understanding. It was sobering to witness when Lise and her mother spoke French to him each evening and to realize that in terms of bilingual comprehension, this terrier was more advanced than I was. (Given what he'd seen of my behavior in the apartment, it was a good thing he couldn't talk, too.)

On the other hand, though it sounds terrible to say so, Papa's terminal illness smoothed the way for my acceptance. The first time I joined Lise and her mother to visit his bedside, where he was completely immobilized, a prisoner of a ghastly array of IVs and tubes, his eyes peered feverishly at me from under their sallow lids. Even through his pain, he was curious. One of the first things he said, which Lise translated for me, was: "*So he's the one?*" There was a pause, then he strained to reach out his hand. He wanted to shake with me. Obviously, I reciprocated. It was a comfort to Monsieur to see that his daughter was not alone—his only child, of whom he was fiercely proud, the object of his adoration and the symbol of the striving of generations: he, the son of a glass-cutter, the first in his family to go to university and to occupy a civil service job, had lived to see his cherished girl continue the family trajectory to the highest levels, for Lise had passed the notoriously difficult entrance exam to one of the most venerated schools in France (passing this exam was an achievement which a small circle of people carried with them for the rest of their lives, a feat which dwarfed more banal adult successes). His daughter kept company with the children of diplomats and went on ski holidays with them, too. His Lise! And now she had chosen her man. When her Papa was gone, his prized girl wouldn't be alone. "*So he's the one?*" His hand rose to reach me. He looked at Lise's mother, Marie-Thérèse, who wasn't about to contradict him: she nodded back. Lise, who in these circumstances would've done anything to please her father, took my other hand and nodded, too. Good old me! I was the man of the hour. The skin on Papa's hand felt like hot, brittle paper; his eyes shone with a drugged burning. I managed this much: "*Oui, c'est moi.*"

———— ✦ ————

Getting my first job in Paris, though, turned out to be tougher than acquiring a family. At first, I was as naive as a newborn chick. I hopped around, expected people to like me, even find me cute. But in Paris, hell, they just pick you up and throw you into a sauce for that night's dinner.

Although my linguistic abilities gradually surpassed Clo-Clo's, it soon became apparent that despite my vigor and my A-minus average at Pizza U, there wasn't much about me that interested Parisian employers, who wanted someone who could engage with people and type French into a computer without risking the ridiculous. There was also the problem of working papers. I'd arrived on a tourist visa. Lise and I planned to get married, which would eventually straighten out my situation, but we had to bury Papa first, then produce reams of personal documents to attest to our backgrounds and good faith and legal residence.

In the meantime, I found an off-the-books job giving English lessons to the staff of a glassware importer in La Courneuve. It was very lowly paid but allowed me to keep up appearances. I was occupied. I troubled no one. It no longer felt like I was bluffing.

Then, at a small but elegant reception arranged by Lise to celebrate her mother's birthday, I had my first public setback. There were a few champagne toasts; next, we sat down to listen to a string quartet perform Vivaldi's "The Four Seasons." This had been a personal favorite of Lise's father, and the performance was also a memorial in his honor, given his absence on this special day.

The musicians plunged in with energy, and though the music was familiar, for I'd heard it in other contexts, I'd never listened to it in its entirety or seen it performed live, in intimate surroundings. The effect was impressive. After the fourth piece, to show my appreciation, I started clapping enthusiastically.

Unfortunately, this was much too soon. Call me stupid, but I hadn't realized that the concerto contained pauses *within* movements, that the seasonal cycle was not yet finished. Instead of the four seasons being over, it was still "Indian Summer" or "Winter Thaw" or some damn thing. Lise and I sat up front, in full view of the guests. Lise grabbed my elbow to stop me, but too late; in sight of the entire assembly, the lead violinist cast me a withering look, lifted his instrument under his chin, then resumed playing. The other musicians jumped in, sawing convulsively: music swelled. It was mortifying. Lise's mother lowered her eyes and stared into her lap, her lips pressed tight. If there is life after death and if from some other sphere Lise's father was watching over us at that moment, his soul twisted and turned and despaired, "*No, no, he's NOT the one!*"

━━ ✦ ━━

During this same period, Lise was offered two very good jobs, one in the staff of a prominent politician, one for a major weekly news magazine. After placing a few phone calls to schoolmates' parents, she opted for the latter. She'd had no training or experience in journalism whatsoever—in fact, to my astonishment, I learned that she'd never held a job before, beyond symbolic internships arranged through her special school—but Lise announced that she preferred the idea of being an influential journalist. Politics had lost much of its luster lately.

We moved to a corner apartment in the 7th arrondissement, a smart one-bedroom that we got with the help of another school connection. We pushed back our wedding date due to paperwork delays, but in other respects, we settled in. Each morning, we planned our day over bowls of coffee.

"Don't forget Hugues and Sylvie," she said.

"Is that tonight?"

We'd been invited to a reception, an early evening pre-dinner affair, at an address on the Boulevard Saint-Germain. These people weren't friends, but they were important for Lise and her work and needed to be cultivated; there would be some famous names there, too, at least well-known faces on television. The reception was to launch a new cable channel.

"Of course it's tonight."

"You have so many of these things. We should spend more time alone."

"Don't be selfish."

"Well, I might be a little late by the time I get back from La Courneuve."

"Just do the best you can."

It was a long commute to the suburbs, and that afternoon there were delays on the RER B train. By the time I got home and took a shower, I wasn't in the best mood. But then, looking in the closet for something to wear to the reception, I spied the leather vest that Lise had bought me back in the States. And I dug more deeply and found the cowboy hat, too. So I rooted around for a few more accessories and tried to deck myself out like in the old days.

Of course, it was a joke, but I wasn't trying to be provocative. It was for *us*, really. Besides, these were media people. My idea was that I'd show up in this garb, which might turn a few heads, and then a little later, Lise and I could eclipse ourselves and go have some fun. Just the two of us.

———— ✦ ————

The lady who opened the door grinned when she saw me, and I smiled back, then followed her across creaking parquetry into a series of high-ceilinged rooms where people mingled with flutes of champagne in their hands, their voices rising and echoing above a background of decorative jazz. From the moment I entered, I received stares.

To anyone whose eyes met mine, I gave a nod. It seemed the best way to carry this off. Besides, I was quick to notice that at least half the men weren't wearing ties, and some of them were unshaven, though admittedly in the calculated fashion of French journalists who want to communicate that they are really intellectuals who scorn journalists. The women were more formally dressed, with jackets and the occasional leather mini skirt. There was one fellow in a sailor suit, munching a canapé—maybe a character on a TV show?—but it was obvious, as I moved through the crowd in search of Lise, that my informality struck a different note.

By now, the door was far behind me; there was no turning back. So I set my jaw. Why should I apologize? I belonged here, too.

"Oh, there you are!"

Lise looked up, startled. These were my first words, interrupting her mid-sentence. I'd spoken in English, whereas she'd been conversing in French.

Her companions turned in my direction. This was Sylvie and Hugues: an Antillaise woman in a dress open down to her navel and a man with red-framed glasses, pencil sideburns, and a skiff hairdo. It seemed to require Lise several seconds to recognize me under my cowboy hat; she leaned back a notch to take me in. She wore tight black jeans with a mustard blouse, one of my favorites, and a mauve embroidered jacket that I didn't recognize. She must've bought it for the occasion. "Hu-hullo," she said.

There was a pause, during which I felt Lise's eyes on me. I plunged into small talk with Sylvie and Hugues because it was easier than returning Lise's gaze. At the same time, my brain was racing. Why this cowboy outfit had seemed, only a short time before, a good move was now a profound mystery. There was a mirror over a mantelpiece to reflect a chandelier in the center of the room, but in it, I could also observe our circle: the backs of

Sylvie and Hugues' heads, Lise, whose mouth had tensed into a flat, crushed bloom, and standing next to her, an asshole in a big hat.

I resolved not to linger. Sylvie and Hugues weren't unfriendly, but after few sentences, I addressed Lise and suggested that it was time to go.

"Go? Now?"

"Yes, you know." I smiled.

"Know what? Go where?"

"I'm sorry," I told Sylvie and Hugues. "Other obligations!"

"I'm not going anywhere," Lise said.

And though I realized that I was in the wrong, a sentimental part of me also believed that she ought to have a little sympathy. Look at the compromising situation I was in! Couldn't she help me out a little here? Even if I was an asshole in a big hat, wasn't I still her fiancé?

I persisted, fabricating an imaginary appointment. Sylvie and Hugues looked on, embarrassed at our bickering. At one point, I turned to them and said, "We have so much paperwork to sort out."

"So go do it!" Lise hissed.

At that moment, something slipped, and a sickly premonition came to me. Our paperwork would never be sorted out. With a forced shrug of shoulders, I excused myself from them and angled back through the crowd, making my way for the door. My face must have looked very grave, for the fellow in the sailor suit suddenly loomed before me and said in English, in a soothing tone, "What's the matter, cowboy?" Wordlessly, I touched the brim of my hat, then found myself on the Boulevard Saint Germain, turning toward the traffic, walking into the sun.

ROCK STARS COME TO ST. INGBERT

C.B. Heinemann

The ancient hamlet of St. Ingbert, hidden away unobtrusively in the middle of Germany, was always an easy gig for us when we traveled around Europe playing music during the summers. Charlie, Drew, and I had managed to snag a series of gigs in a chain of Irish pubs set up by the Guinness Corporation all over Germany, and St. Ingbert was home to one of the more pleasant ones. It was set in a shady corner of the central pedestrian zone, the crowds were appreciative, the staff was friendly, the beer was excellent, and we merely had to stagger upstairs to our rooms rather than attempt to drive anywhere at the end of the night.

While playing a gig one cool September evening, we noticed a group of guys coming in the door on the other side of the room, and a collective gasp ran through the room. I glanced over at Charlie, who sat on his stool playing the uilleann pipes and nodded their way. He looked up and squinted, shrugging his shoulders. As the song ended, I noticed people muttering something to each other that I couldn't make out. I then turned to Drew on guitar, who also had his eyes fixed on the newcomers. "What's the deal with these guys?" I asked, away from the microphone.

Drew looked at me with a huge smile, and I could have sworn his glasses steamed up. "It's Nazareth."

"Nazareth? What's that supposed to mean? It's not Christmas or anything."

He shook his head. "No, man. Nazareth. You know, the band. Nazareth."

"I think I've heard of them."

He screwed his face up at me. "You think you've heard of them? Come on, man. 'Love Hurts,' 'Hair of the Dog.' Nazareth.

They're here. This is incredible."

"I doubt they're in Saint Ingbert." I looked at my setlist. "Whoever they are, we've still got a gig to play. Let's get going. Let's do 'Cold Rain.'"

"Oh man, I can't believe this," Drew gushed. "I'd know them anywhere. Nazareth, here, seeing us. I can't . . ."

"Worry about it later, ready? Three, four . . ."

We played through our set, but I couldn't help feeling a bit more self-conscious than usual. I occasionally looked over at their table to see if I could gauge their reaction. I barely knew of them, but hell, if everybody was right, they were genuine rock stars. Nobody in the audience bothered to pay any attention to us. Rock stars had come to St. Ingbert!

As we neared the end of our set, my self-consciousness ballooned. I could hardly wait to get off the stage and out of earshot of the "stars." We probably sounded like crap to them, I imagined. But once we got off the stage, they would no doubt feel obliged to come over and introduce themselves. I was mortified, wishing they hadn't come at all, and we could have just had a normal night without the audience murmuring at each other, looking at the stars, and without me feeling every flub and misplaced note or chord slash at my heart like a machete.

As soon as we started to leave the stage, I saw them get up and make their way through the crowd over to us. It seemed we were about to meet the Rock Stars. I could tell by his quivering "Oh man" that Drew was about to pop. Charlie, as always, was oblivious.

One of them, a lean, older guy with a bush of slightly graying hair, patted me on the shoulder. "Good job, lads, grand stuff," he said in a raspy Scottish accent, his eyes mischievous. "We had no idea they were having music here tonight—we just came for a few jars. This is a bit of luck for us. I'm Dan, by the way."

"We know who you are, and this is way more than a bit of luck for us," Drew blurted. "You guys are Nazareth."

The big guy with a shaved head laughed. "Yeah, so we've heard. So, you must know I'm Pete. Pete Agnew."

"Thanks for coming down," I said uncertainly. "Quite an honor."

Dan grinned benevolently. "The honor is all ours. Come, let's have a drink."

"A good few drinks, I would think," said the third guy. He looked younger than the others, had long, dark hair, and wore a black leather jacket.

"What brings you to Saint Ingbert?" Drew asked. "Not exactly the middle of the universe here."

"There's a lovely recording studio here in town run by a guy we know," said Dan. "We're recording our next album here and taking a little holiday. What are you lads doing here? You're a lot further from home than we are."

"That's a long story," I said. "Years ago, we came here to busk just for fun. Then we started getting gigs, and now we come every year to play."

"So this is how you spend your summer holidays?" Dan laughed. "I like it."

Billy leaned closer. "Would you lads mind if we do a couple of numbers during your break? And play your guitars?"

Drew nearly leaped out of his chair. "Are you kidding? That would be awesome! You can play my guitar, no problem. I can't believe this."

"Yeah, you can play my guitar, too," I said, becoming a little bit infected by Drew's enthusiasm. "It would be great to hear you."

Pete laughed. "And don't worry, Charlie. We won't touch your pipes."

"Speaking of the pipes," said Dan with one finger raised. "We'd like to talk to you about that."

Billy stood up. "After we play. Come on, let's do it."

The three of them headed for the stage. I followed them in

case they needed help with the sound system. I could hear the audience let out a second communal gasp. Billy grabbed my 12-string, examined my tone settings for a second, then turned them all up all the way. "Sorry, but fuck your tones," he said with a laugh. "I just turn up everything all the way."

Moments later, Dan stepped to his microphone. "Hello, everybody. We're Nazareth."

While the crowd howled with disbelief and excitement, the three sang the chorus to "The Long Black Veil" in perfect harmony. They sounded fantastic. When the guitars came in, I could tell right away—these guys were the real thing, total pros. They even looked more like rock stars than before, though they had more of a country sound on acoustic instruments.

After "Long Black Veil," they went right into another song and then another. Not rockers, but folk songs, sung in those pristine harmonies. The crowd pushed to the edge of the stage. I had to admit, they were tight and professional and obviously having a good time. And to be honest, they sounded a lot better than we did.

I felt a hand on my shoulder. "This is worth the whole trip over, man," said Drew. "I can't believe this. Hanging out with Nazareth. It's like a dream."

When at last they left the stage, the audience moved closer to shake their hands and get autographs. The bartenders loaded our table with pints of beer, and the manager—a guy of about twenty-three from Dublin with thinning blond hair and a generally sour expression—glided over, his face flushed. "This has been a brilliant night, lads, just brilliant. Take the rest of the night off, and don't worry, you'll be getting your full pay."

Nazareth sat back at the table and drained their pints while shaking a few last hands. Dan leaned over the table at us. "What I was hoping to ask is if we could borrow your piper for the rest of the night? Charlie, would you mind coming over to the studio and laying down a pipe track on one of our songs? We'll pay you, of course."

"Sure, why not?" Charlie was nonplussed.

"Yeah, just like a few seconds during an instrumental break on this song we've been working on. Shouldn't take long. You can all come along, of course."

Pete was beaming. "Yeah, those pipes will be just what the break needs." He pumped his elbow and pretended to play the pipes himself while emitting a groaning sound. "Yeah, friggin' magic!"

Billy looked around at us. "Let's finish our pints first, lads. Pleasure before business, right?"

As we drank, Drew squeezed my arm. "Oh man, I'm going to piss myself! Now we're going into the studio with them, and Charlie's gonna be on their next album! Is this wild or what? Can you believe this? Can you?"

"I guess I'd better."

Many strange and unexpected things happened during our little European tours, so I didn't feel quite as blown away as Drew did—it was just the latest in a long string of adventures. In a way. In another way, it was on a different level. After all, Charlie really was recording with Nazareth. Who knows, I thought, it may turn out to be a big hit song, and there's our Charlie blasting away on his pipes!

We finished up and headed out the door while a few straggling fans smiled at us and waved. "We're parked in this blue van right out front," said Dan. "Where are you parked?"

"Just around the corner."

"All right, we'll wait for you. Give us a honk when you're behind us."

We followed their van through the streets and out into the countryside to a large one-story stone building surrounded by bushes and gardens. We parked in front of a big glass door and followed Nazareth into a nearly bare interior with white wall-to-wall carpeting and a few chairs. Dan led us around a corner and opened two black wooden doors into a darkened recording studio where rock music roared from speakers on the wall. All we could see were little red lights, illuminated dials, and a guy with a short beard smoking a cigarette and leaning over a soundboard glittering with sliders, dials, knobs, and lights.

Pete turned to Drew and me. "That's Darrell, our drummer, doing the mixing tonight. All right, lads, we're going to get Charlie all set up in the sound booth right now. Billy, show these other lads where you can have a few beers in the meantime."

Somehow, a few others from the pub—two young waitresses from Ireland and an inebriated American guy named Jack Brandon who played the same circuit of pubs we did and was visiting on his night off—had managed to join us. Billy showed us into a cozy little room with a refrigerator, three big sofas, some chairs, and a large table. Billy grabbed handfuls of German beers from the fridge and handed them out while we sat down. "Okay," he said with a big goofy smile. "How about we have a bit of a singsong, right? I've got my guitar right over here."

He pulled an acoustic guitar from a closet and led us through several songs without a pause between them. He started with "Can't Buy Me Love" by the Beatles, an Irish folk song I didn't know, "Blowin' in the Wind," "My Bonnie Lies over the Ocean," and some Christmas songs. He and Pete sang with such unselfconscious gusto that I had to laugh. So this is what rock stars are really like, I thought. Maybe the key to their success is simply extreme enthusiasm.

After that, we all sat around talking. Billy told us that he was the new guy in the band and was still learning their songs. "I'm having the best time of my life right now, to be honest. I hope it never ends."

"Yeah, he's only about twenty, but he's good," said Pete. "Me, I'm over forty now, but you know what?" He turned to me with eyes wide and a huge, toothy smile. "I don't give a damn! I'm having a good time, and I don't care what anybody thinks."

We chatted and sang a few more songs while the beer continued to flow. Jack asked Pete about how Nazareth got their start while Billy played some nice blues guitar. The two waitresses who had joined us were very young and pretty, and I wondered if anyone would make a move on them. Nobody said or did anything inappropriate. Our rock stars were quite well-behaved.

At last, Billy jumped to his feet. "Come on, lads, let's go see how the recording's coming along. They should be done by now."

As we entered the recording studio to the ear-splitting sound of Nazareth's latest song blasting from the speakers, Billy and Pete started dancing along to the music. Over at the soundboard, Dan was bopping along, clapping his hands, and shouting encouragement at Charlie, who we could see through the Plexiglas of an isolated sound booth wailing away on his pipes. Darrell didn't move.

Billy, Pete, and Dan danced around the room with huge smiles. They obviously loved their own sound, which might be another key to their success.

As the song ended, Dan shouted to Charlie. "All right, brilliant, so let's do it one more time, only this time with emphasis on the two and four, right? Diddle diddle DAH, diddle diddle DAH, right? Just do that just like that, right? One more time."

The engineer cued up the tape while Dan turned to us. "It's a bit of a job getting him to play exactly what we want, but he's getting there."

We sat around while Charlie went over and over the short break and Dan gestured at him through the window. Jack Brandon sat next to Darrell and asked him about the various knobs and dials. Billy went to the door. "Come on, you lot. Let's leave them to it and have a few more beers."

We followed him back to our assigned room. It was getting very late, and I was wearing down. As we opened one last beer, Dan came in with Charlie. "All right, lads, it's all done. Let's have one last beer and get some rest. Thanks, Charlie."

Everyone was exhausted, and even Drew had had enough. At last, following the directions of the two waitresses from the pub, we drove back. Charlie was at the wheel because the rest of us could still feel the beer sloshing around inside us. We assumed that our big night with the Rock Stars was over.

Not quite. The next morning, we staggered down from our sleeping area into the dimly lit pub, where a few customers sat having coffee. One of them was Jack Brandon. "I've been waiting for you guys."

"Hey, what's up?" I asked.

He gave us an embarrassed smirk. "I left my jacket at the studio last night and wondered if you could give me a ride over. I don't have a car."

"Sure, no problem."

He looked away, and his smirk twisted into something else. "There might be a little bit of a problem."

"What's that?"

"Well, I, ah, had an accident when we were there."

"What do you mean?"

After a pause, he sighed. "I barfed all over the soundboard."

"You did what?"

"Yeah, you heard right. I was pissed out of my head and tossed my cookies right there, right on that damned soundboard."

Drew's eyes nearly shot out of his head and hit the opposite wall. "Oh my God, that board is worth thousands, Jack. Did they see you do it?"

"Oh yeah, and I gave them about three hundred dollars, too. For cleaning."

"Oh, this is just great." I realized that now we'd have to present ourselves to the Rock Stars, and because of Jack, we would not be the most popular Americans in that section of Germany. "Come on, let's get it over with."

"I've got to go there anyway to get my check," said Charlie. "I hope they still give it to me."

We managed to find our way back and knocked on the door. Dan opened it with bloodshot eyes and looked us over. "Oh, right, there you are." His voice was rough from cigarettes. "Here."

He let us in the entry, handed Jack his jean jacket and Charlie his check. "Quite a night we had last night, wasn't it?"

"Man, I'm so sorry about the mixing board," Jack began. "If you need any more money, or maybe I can come in and clean it again myself."

Dan shook his head. "It'll be fine. Not the first time something like this has happened. So look, we'll see you around, right?"

And that was it.

Events quickly demanded attention to other issues. We had a long, hot drive to our next gig. Charlie and Drew, who had never gotten along, stopped speaking to each other and nearly came to blows one night in Heidelberg. I caught a terrible cold and had to take two nights off, leaving the stage to two guys who by then hated each other. The van broke down. Then it broke down again. By the time our tour finally ended after two tense nights at The Irish Rover Pub in Charlemagne's former capital of Aachen, nobody was thinking about our night with the rock stars.

Years later, while driving up Interstate 95 in Maryland, a Nazareth song come on the radio. I recognized it immediately and nearly ran off the road. I had to pull over at a gas station to listen—it was the song Charlie played on. During the instrumental break, I leaned closer and could just barely hear, behind the wash of guitars and drums, that diddle-diddle-DAH of Charlie's pipes. Our night with the Rock Stars had been immortalized forever.

THE ISLAND THAT TIME FORGOT

Steve Slavin

When someone tells you, "This is a true story," you'd probably be right to assume that they're lying through their teeth. So, I won't blame you if you don't believe a word of what you're about to read....

———— ✦ ————

In 1971, I made arrangements with the International Planned Parenthood Association to spend three months in Barbados, where I would study the work of the Barbados Family Planning Association. Barbados stood out among all the Caribbean nations in reducing its birth rate in recent years, and their great success appeared to be an excellent topic for my doctoral dissertation at New York University.

Like many American graduate students, I had shoulder-length hair and a full beard. I often wore "conquistador shirts" with puffy sleeves, open to the navel, and a silver chain around my neck, anchored by an intricate silver peace medallion shaped like an upside-down letter "Y."

Back then, passengers taking international flights out of Newark Airport often lined up on the tarmac before boarding. It was about seven on a beautiful May morning, with the sun well above the horizon. I was in a great mood, thinking that in another year or two, I would have "Doctor" placed before my name.

There was a very serious-looking man in a business suit, carefully examining everyone in the line. When someone looked at least a little bit "off" to him, he would nod, and the person would step out of the line. Before his eyes fell on me, I stepped out of line on my own.

The man broke into a big grin, barely able to restrain himself from laughing. I was grinning too. We had had a complete meeting of the minds. After asking me a few perfunctory questions, he directed me to get back in line, calling after me, "Good luck with your research!"

I took this to be a very good omen. Having been up most of the night, I managed to catch a few hours of sleep on the flight. After changing planes in Puerto Rico, I finally arrived in Barbados in the early evening.

——— ✦ ———

I spent my first night in a hotel — a luxury no impoverished graduate student could afford for very long. The next day, I made my way to the headquarters of the Barbados Family Planning Association, located in the heart of Bridgetown, the nation's capital.

Lionel Gilkes, the manager, warmly welcomed me, pronouncing that all of the BFPA's data was at my disposal. Just across the way, some Canadian demographers, with newly minted PhDs, were at work on a cushy research project financed by the Rockefeller Foundation.

Lionel approached one of the young Bajan clerical workers and asked her if she would like to look at his "banana."

She smilingly replied that she had no interest in tiny plantains. I had quickly gained an insight into the Island's culture: Its social currency was dirty jokes. Suffice it to say that I had arrived well equipped.

Lionel was friendly with a major contributor to the BFPA, who rented me a small apartment for very affordable rent. It was in Christ Church, just a four-mile bike ride from Bridgetown's downtown.

I moved in that afternoon and then went swimming at Accra Beach, which was within easy walking distance. A very friendly Australian expatriate, Bob, the proprietor of Bob's Beach Shak, sold me a ten-year-old English racer for about twenty-five dollars, and I was now in business.

The title of my dissertation, although rather pretentious sounding, provides a good indication of the work I had cut out for myself: *An Evaluation of the Economic Cost and Effectiveness of the Barbados Family Planning Association.*

I got a tremendous head start by turning up every morning at the BFPA Headquarters and poring over their data. But I also needed data from half a dozen government departments, mainly from their annual reports. Mercifully, most were twenty or thirty pages of statistical tables, which only bureaucrats and impoverished doctoral students could appreciate.

The only problem was that some of the departments had fallen about seven years behind, so in 1971, the year of my visit, they would show me annual reports from around 1964. Very strange.

Still, most of the department heads, or their seconds-in-command, promised to provide me with more recent reports fresh off the press. I could pick these up before I went back to New York.

Another peculiar thing I noticed was that the Island's television programming also seemed strangely out of date. At the time, there was just one TV channel serving the Island, and, as I biked by homes, I often heard reruns of "I Love Lucy" and "The Honeymooners." I realized that anyone who wanted to catch up on fifties TV should move to Barbados.

Barbados is a very small country, about fourteen miles wide at its widest point and twenty-one miles long. When I had been there for a few weeks, I arranged an interview with the Commissioner of Welfare, Clyde Gollup. He held two other government titles – which I can no longer recall – so we arranged to spend some of our time driving from one place to another.

Clyde was a very pleasant and easygoing man, and as we drove along in his open-air land rover, he was constantly waving to people he knew. Then, he confided, by way of explanation, "We live in a very small country."

When we arrived at our final destination, a child daycare center, we were greeted by two older women, and the four of us sat down at a card table outside the center. Clyde was there to accept a donation of toys from one of the center's benefactors.

I had mentioned to Clyde that one of the jobs I held soon after college was with the New York City Department of Welfare. With very little training and no previous experience, newly minted "Social Investigators" visited the homes of welfare recipients largely to ensure that their basic needs were being met and that they were paying their rent and utility bills.

To pass the time, I readily indulged in one of the country's favorite social activities, telling my companions a series of dirty jokes. Soon we were all laughing uproariously. Meanwhile, a photographer was roving around, taking pictures. The next day, two of her photos were displayed on the first page of *The Advocate*, the island's four-page daily newspaper.

The caption below one photo was, "Welfare Commissioner Clyde Gollup receives toys for daycare center from (donor's name)." The other photo caught me with my arms thrust into the air, laughing with my three companions, two of whom were identified as Assistant Commissioners of Welfare.

But more than that photo, what really caught my attention was the banner headline across the top of the page, "Welfare Expert Visits Island." My first thought was of what my supervisor at the Welfare Department, Mrs. Cunningham, would have thought of the headline.

Perhaps, because Barbados was a very small country, the editors of *The Advocate* might have coined the motto, "All the news that could fit on four pages." That would appear to be the only way to explain how an exchange of "Letters to the Editor" merited first-page banner headlines.

The summer of 1971 was quite memorable because of the release of the Pentagon Papers by Daniel Ellsberg, a U.S. Defense Department official. An internally prepared a top-secret study of the history of the American involvement in the Vietnam War, this 7,000-page document was not just made public but was printed by *The New York Times* and *The Washington Post.*

A guy named Barret kicked off our debate with a long letter to the editor, attacking Ellsberg for revealing a top-secret document. The next day the great debate spilled over to the first page with my reply, which defended Ellsberg's actions.

Back and forth, we went for about a week. I can't remember which of us quit first, but for the rest of my stay on the Island, *The Advocate* would remain silent on this *issue*. I'd like to think that just like the Lincoln-Douglas debates stand out in American history, the Island's future historians will similarly recall the Barret-Slavin debates.

———— ✦ ————

Within a few weeks after arriving, I had learned that Bajans considered themselves the most British of all the citizens in the Commonwealth Caribbean.

Even more than the Jamaicans and the Guyanese – citizens of former British Guyana – they revered their connection to the former Motherland. Indeed, Barbados certainly had its share of nobility, such as Sir Frank Knight and Lady Adams. Lionel Gilkes often proudly proclaimed he was a "Britisher."

One day I insisted that I too had a touch of nobility.

"And what is that, my friend?"

"My full name and title is Steve Slavin, OBE." The Order of the British Empire is relatively low honor given to individuals not holding hereditary peerages."

Lionel burst out laughing and called, then called over Mr. Gittens, a retired government official who had been pensioned off with what appeared to be a make-work clerical job.

"Did you hear *that*, Mr. Gittens?"

"Hear what?" he asked, cupping his ear.

"Our friend says that he is an OBE."

The two of them enjoyed a good laugh over this. Then Mr.

Gittens decided to lower the boom.

"Steve," I may be just an old fool, but even I know they don't give OBEs to people from Brooklyn."

After Lionel finally stopped laughing, he invited me to join him and his good friend Zach in a nearby rum shop. Zach was a newspaper reporter from Guyana, and I was curious to get his take on Barbados.

An hour later, Zach and Lionel had more than a dozen empty beer bottles lined up in front of them, while I had three or four empty bottles of nonalcoholic ginger beer.

When I asked Josh about the stories he was working on, he explained that it was hard to keep track of all of them.

"How many stories *are* you working on."

"Seventeen."

"I can't believe that you can possibly be working on so many stories simultaneously."

"That is an excellent observation. Perhaps the actual number is twenty-two." I wondered if one of them was the Barrett-Slavin debate.

In the meanwhile, Lionel had been greeting every woman entering the rum shop – young or old – with the same question: "Can you tell me the definition of a 'yarfoe?'" Invariably they would smile or even laugh, but no one took the bait.

After a while, Zach noticed my confused look and explained that a yarfoe was a rooster who serviced the hens. He laughed when he saw my "Ah hah!" expression, as it finally dawned upon me what Lionel was up to.

Finally, one young woman came into the shop, and Lionel asked *her* the question. She was smiling, and as she patted him on the shoulder, she said he was indeed a yarfoe. But sadly, he had gotten so old that he could not remember that he was.

Lionel stumbled to his feet, bowed to the young woman, and said, "Thank you! You have given me the best answer I have gotten all evening."

I was very pleased with my visit so far, but I began to worry about getting up-to-date annual reports from the Department of Statistics and other government departments. The only organization that had had completely up-to-the-minute data was the Barbados Family Planning Association. That data was crucial to my dissertation because I would be attempting to measure the effectiveness of that organization on reducing the Island's birth rate.

About ten days before I returned to New York, I made the rounds of the government departments that had promised me updated annual reports. The Minister of the Department of Statistics handed me a manilla envelope, as did the Ministers of three other agencies.

When I got back to my apartment, I opened each envelope. And sure enough, each department had, as promised, provided me with updated annual reports. In fact, I may have been holding the largest stash of 1965 annual reports on the entire island.

***

Every Saturday afternoon, I walked to Accra Beach and hung out with a bunch of other expatriates and some Bajans as well. Having been on the Island for three months, I was almost a regular at these gatherings. Toward the end of my stay, a woman who worked at the University of the West Industries invited me to a lecture by the Barbados Ambassador to the Organization of American States.

It was scheduled the next Friday at eight p.m. and would be followed by a reception. I well knew by now that Friday night was the night that many people liked to drink.

I had not brought an extensive wardrobe from New York, but I did wear my favorite conquistador shirt. I hadn't trimmed my hair or beard in at least six months, so I looked even more exotic than I had when I arrived on the Island.

I arrived halfway through the lecture, thoroughly drenched

by an extremely heavy downpour. My friend got me a few towels, and by the time the reception began, the rum and beer were flowing freely. Because I had a relatively long bike ride home, I settled for ginger beer.

Finally, close to midnight, I coasted down the steep hill from the campus to the deserted two-lane highway, which I hoped would take me back to Bridgetown. The road was unlit, and my bike light flashed no more than fifteen feet in front of me.

What if I had turned off the hill and had gone in the wrong direction? It was still drizzling, and I grew increasingly worried about ending up in the sugar cane fields.

But then, I began seeing an increasing number of lights. The rain was finally letting up. That had to be Bridgetown up ahead, so I knew I would get home in one piece.

After riding that distance, I noticed that my shirt, which was a bit too tight, had unbuttoned, and my peace medallion was in prominent display. I rode along, arms extended outward, with my palms up to feel the cool mist hanging in the air. I was in a great mood, very pleased with everything I had managed to accomplish on my dissertation research while thoroughly enjoying myself on the Island.

Now I just needed to get my bearings and find the highway leading to Christ Church. As I slowly rode through the streets of Bridgetown, I passed through one that looked very familiar.

It was the infamous Baxter's Lane, lined with honkytonks, rum shops, and bars. Hundreds of people, apparently quite inebriated, were hanging around on the sidewalks and out in the street. The only traffic was me on my bike.

I was still riding with no hands. My arms were still extended outward with my palms up as I continued feeling the mist. Feeling a bit more adventurous, I even began to tilt my face upward so that I could better embrace the mist.

And then, something very strange began to happen. People started pointing at me. Several people were making the sign of the cross. Some of them actually got down on their knees. All these poor souls were having this weird religious experience.

Suddenly, something behind me flashed so brightly that I could see my shadow on the pavement. Then, suddenly, I had a vision. It was the front page of tomorrow's *Advocate*.

There was a huge photograph of a man with long hair and a full beard. He was riding down Baxter's Lane, his face tilted upward, arms stretched out to the side, his palms turned upward. The banner headline was just three words long: "Savior Visits Island."

CHILE PASTE

Robert Beveridge

He sits on the one unburnt piece
of the top step of what was once
a porch, penknife atoms away
from the ball of his thumb over
and over again as the hunk of balsa
in his had becomes a flamingo.
He looks up every once in a while,
towards the trees across the water.
"Sixty-two it was, or sixty-three," spit
in their direction, the brown wad well
short of its target. "Just come
right out of the woods at midnight
when they thought everyone
would be asleep. Crossed the crick
and I don't know what they were after
but from the looks of 'em it was shoes
and a hot meal. Only place you
can see from the river is mine, though,
and I guess they didn't like
what they saw when they peeked
through the window. By the time
I got outside with the shotgun
they'd lit some branches
and caught the back corner
of the porch. Gave me enough
light to wing one, I think, as they
headed on towards town. You
see any bodies wearin' grey
on the way out here?" I stopped

the recorder on my smartphone,
shook my head. The trees, too,
remained silent on the far shore.

LIKE BATS

Robert Beveridge

You have a vision
of fruit jets, tell me
about grape fighters
over Lebanon, kiwis
on carriers and
supersonic apricots.
I ask you if you
remember Venice
the breeze that made
a walk indistinguishable
from a thunderstorm.
We spent our days under
awnings, in stores
that wrapped our meager
purchases in plastic.
It didn't matter. Books,
cutlets, jewelry all
waterlogged when we
arrived back at our pension.

Still, it was exercise. Neither
of us could read Italian,
anyway, and we cook
for vegetarians. Hurry,
our banana awaits,
gondolier's foot a-tap-tap-
tap on the cobblestones.

THE FOREST OF SIGNS

K.C. Wolfe

One morning, at a truck stop on the Alaska Highway, a bearded man poked his head through our open window and asked if we needed any smokes.

Sarah and I were in our early twenties then. Earlier that summer, we had left the only home either one of us had known—Upstate New York—and were driving to Alaska because we were young and in love. We had left home, I think, because I thought I maybe had to and because she was certain of it.

I squinted at the man. Middle-thirties, fleshy, hirsute, with unruly reddish hair that matched his beard in both hue and length. I had already been leaning toward the knife in the door's pocket and came up with a pack of Players cigarettes. "We're good," I said, shaking them in front of him. "We have plenty."

He smiled a cautious smile with mustard-colored teeth. He took a step back from the car, looked around, and leaned back in. "No, I mean *smoke*. Grass. You guys want some grass?"

Sarah and I shared a look. I'm not sure what mine communicated; probably fatigue. We had spent a sleepless night in the car the night before. Her look said: yeah, come on, idiot.

"Give us a second?" I asked. The man nodded. He stepped back from the window and squinted into the sun as if checking the time.

"We're not taking it over the border," I said.

"No shit."

"But we have two days before worrying about that."

"It's not like we're gonna get pulled over."

"And we're in B.C."

She looked out into the gray parking lot and up into the boughs of spruce above. "I think we're in the Yukon," she said.

153

"Just get a bit. I have to pee."

"Sure," I said to the bearded man.

Sarah went to the truck stop, and I locked the car and followed the man. He pointed at an RV sitting on the edge of the lot twenty yards from us, where another RV and two dust-covered pickups sat empty—one with Alberta tags and the other from Texas. I looked back to the truck stop and noticed its sign for the first time: Contact Creek Lodge. Sixty-three years before, a U.S. Army regiment working south met their counterparts working north and linked the bush trails that would become the only highway to Alaska. They named the place.

The man's RV looked to be from the late eighties, faded beige with graying stripes, the kind with the pickup cab built-in like a cube truck. His plates said *Beautiful British Columbia*. His clothes—baggy corduroy trousers, a thermal shirt, an aged winter vest—said laid back. He walked a body length ahead with a slight limp and with his face mostly to the ground, coming up occasionally to look at me and speak, the creases of his mouth beginning to spread, but nothing coming out.

We entered the RV through a small door on the side. The innards were the same faded beige as the paint job. It smelled musty and stale but appeared neatly tended. A bunk hung from the wall covered in a strangle of wool blankets. A dozen broken-spined paperbacks lined a shelf behind a guardrail, like on a sailboat. Naturalist titles: plants, flowers, trails. An odd smattering of novels: Louis L'Amour, Margaret Atwood, *Zen and the Art of Motorcycle Maintenance*.

"How much you thinking?" he asked.

"Like ten, Canadian?"

He nodded, expressionless, maybe disappointed. He unlatched and opened a cabinet. Shielded by the open door, he reached into what I imagined was an enormous bag of B.C. grass.

Could I live like this, alone on the road, wandering? Maybe. A part of me could. But he seemed lonely, not lonesome, and not the lonely where you're dying to talk to someone and gab breathlessly to get it out, but the lonely where you don't know how to talk to strangers, where you've lost that, forgotten. Our silence hung like fog, punctuated only by his hand shuffling inside the cabinet.

"Where you headed?" I asked.

"South," he said.

"Is that home?"

He laughed. "I guess."

I didn't get it then. The RV wafted suddenly in a smell like ripe skunk. He held a large pinch of a cannabis bud out, dropped it in my open hand, and asked if that was good. God, it stunk, like the deepest of deep pine forests, obnoxious in its vigor. I took the cellophane from my cigarettes, wrapped the bud up, and put it into my jeans pocket. I handed over a tenner.

"Where you guys headed?" he asked, suddenly more comfortable.

"North," I said and pointed.

———— ✦ ————

While I bought grass, Sarah used the bathroom and bought two burnt coffees in 16-ounce Styrofoam tumblers. A man on a motorcycle pulled up and killed the engine as she walked out of the truck stop. He was in his sixties, clad in blue biker gear—leather jacket, chaps, helmet. He dismounted from a blue Harley Davidson towing a matching blue trailer with New York plates.

"You from New York?" Sarah asked, pointing to the tags.

"Queens," the man said in a downstate accent.

They talked, these New Yorkers. The man—his name was Roger—had ridden his Harley from Queens with a friend headed to Alaska. "The wife says I oughta do it before she won't let me, so here I am," he said. "She wants me home by September, meaning I'm gonna have to turn around the second I cross the border. You believe that?" He looked off, northbound up the road, as if the border where he would turn lay just beyond the bend. "You married?" he asked.

155

"No," Sarah said.

"Well, really, it's great. I'm married thirty years, but you gotta get away from each other sometimes. Some space, you know? Not a bad thing."

Roger had been on the road a month, avoiding caribou collisions, sitting out deluges beneath overpasses, and swilling beers with eccentrics at roadhouse bars. Had she seen the bison? Bears? How beautiful this place was? For him, like us, Canada had been where the continent grew wild.

"I guess this is my mid-life crisis," Roger said.

"I really hope it's not ours," Sarah said.

When I arrived in front of the truck stop, fingering the cellophane bag in my pocket, Sarah was telling Roger how we'd ended up just shy of the Yukon border. She raised and lowered the Styrofoam cups in a pantomime of talking with her hands: fleeing New York, a layover in Colorado, a fiasco at the border, the open-ended destination. Her story was built on a series of places, and these places sounded as if they had happened to us, not us to them.

"Roger," Roger said and extended a gloved hand to me. "You been in the car together all this time?"

"I don't think we've spent more than an hour apart in two months," I said. He laughed, and I wondered if he could smell the bud wrapped up in my pocket. It was all I could smell.

"God. My wife and I woulda been at each other's throats. Now, if I get sick of my buddy here"—he pointed to a motorcyclist rumbling into the dusty parking lot, thirty yards away—"I just throttle it up and lose him."

"He's from New York," Sarah said to me.

"Queens," Roger said. "You?"

"Upstate," I said, "Syracuse."

"I don't know how anyone lives up there." Typical downstate response. He opened his arms to embrace the parking lot. "Or here. Weather like this lasts about two weeks."

I liked Roger. He resembled Peter Boyle in both appearance and peculiarity and reminded me of about twenty people I'd known, metro New Yorkers who had never seen much reason to leave the city and perhaps never had, who regarded driving two hours Upstate as space travel.

I imagined we would see Roger dismount at truck stops over the next two days, and the three of us would sit down and compare notes. We'd keep the same pace. The farther we got from New York, the more we'd find we had in common. In Whitehorse, we'd meet him in the lobby of a hotel and, over beers, figure out that we knew some of the same people.

"I'm a cliché," Roger said, apropos of nothing. "But you two got something going."

Sarah and I considered this for a moment, looking at our feet atop the gray crushed stone of the parking lot. Then she looked up at me as if to check if I agreed.

"Anyway," Roger said, "if you see a blue Harley on the side of the road with no rider, stop and look for my body."

———— ✦ ————

South of Watson Lake, and north of a sign that said WELCOME TO YUKON: LARGER THAN LIFE, we pulled off from the highway along a short track that ran to an isolated pond. This may have been at or near a place called Lucky Lake, Alaska Highway Mile 612. One could barely see the highway from the shore, masked as it was through a copse of shadowy Tim Burton-esque spruce. We dethroned and stretched, and I unrolled the tobacco from a cigarette and meticulously twisted up a bit of the bud.

"Good shit," Sarah said, drawing the smoke in and stifling a cough. I bent over, hacking, feeling a rock form in the pit of my stomach.

"Maybe we'll save the rest of this," I said, hoarse, catching my breath.

"Lightweight," she said.

The pond we parked at stretched deep blue and lily-choked for ten spruce-lined acres.

"You think we'll see Roger again?"

"It's one road," I said. "Of course we'll see Roger."

One RCMP patrol car—the first we'd seen in a week—passed during our speed limit-observing northward crawl to Watson Lake, YT, pop. 1,800. Watson Lake is home to a thrilling Northern Lights simulator, like a planetarium, so one may be awed by the Aurora during months when it operates unseen due to daylight. We missed that. Still stoned, we missed a lot but found, in Watson Lake, an afternoon to wander outside of the car. We strolled around town under bright skies and popped into a hardware store/tackle shop for a canister of stove fuel, a voyage that, under normal circumstances, would take five minutes but which took us twenty. We chatted up the grizzled shopkeeper until Sarah's giggles took over. When we returned to the car, the sky had gone steel, and the rain drizzled so lightly that the water felt as if it hovered mid-air.

The most notable attraction in Watson Lake is The Watson Lake Signpost Forest, which lies at the confluence of the Alaska and Campbell Highways, one of the few true intersections on the road. We did not miss the Signpost Forest, which began when a nostalgic U.S. Army private put up a sign for his hometown of Danville, Illinois, during the building of the highway. The forest has since grown, folks adding sign upon sign, hauling them up from far-off hometowns and attaching them, one atop another, to poles and boards sticking up from the ground. The latest counts put the number of signs north of 70,000.

I think it's safe to say that the Signpost Forest was curated: clean lines of telephone poles arranged in rows like the tidy forests one finds at research stations and logging rehabs. The signs represented every species of worldwide town, village, border, city, and neighborhood: *Koln* and *Kerns*, *Zetel* and *Solingen*, *Winfield* and *Whittier*, *Santa Clarita* and *Harrisonville, MD*, *Entering*

Hardin and *Buckhead City Limit* and *Brookfield, Wisconsin 2269 miles*. Many were cast in the weathered Pine green common to American street signs or in Royal blue or daffodil yellow or white with blue or black letters. Some were messages, hand-painted and home-crafted, commemorating biker reunions and extended family voyages (The O'Hara Clan! 1995!) and cross-continental pilgrimages for the remaining members of a sorority or Vietnam War platoon.

Photos of servicemen next to makeshift signs indicating how far they were from Lowell, Gainesville, or Eufaula are common in the highway build's historical record. And signs like these are especially prevalent in the far north, where municipally funded announcements seem compulsively listed on monuments and posts from Dawson Creek to Barrow. There's one in Fairbanks and downtown Anchorage, and there's one in Alert, in Nunavut, the northernmost populated place in the world. But they are common to other isolated, far-flung places too, like on the long wooden pier in Busselton in Western Australia or in Key West, where a wooden post in the old seaport features a few dozen salt-chewed, hand-painted signs asserting distances to the likes of Wrentham, Massachusetts. Whence does this desire to point and indicate toward one's homeplace come? Who are the pilgrims with the foresight to steal a street sign from Wrentham and haul it to Watson Lake? And how, precisely, did homesickness drive Carl Lindley of the 341st Engineers to signal the name and approximate distance to his obscure Midwestern homeland?

I wasn't sure then, but it felt—as it does now—right. The gesture of hauling and putting up the signs made emotional sense. Perhaps Lindley's point was simply to say: Yes, I am a long way from home. And that desire to point back, to indicate where we've come from, hits on some universal stirring of the soul. Perhaps the signs reach back across the great distances to those places, those homes populated with people who, in our wanderings, we've lost and say: You're still a part of me. Or simply: I miss you.

I ambled through the forest in the feeble drizzle, hoping to find a sign that read SYRACUSE 3,272 MILES. Sarah ambled in her own direction, looking for her own signs. One could get lost in The Signpost Forest, making it feel somewhat like a forest, and after a while, we both did. The signs on their posts rose, wall-like, all around. For the afternoon, we wandered by ourselves, lost and searching. Later, when she recognized a name—"Buffalo!"—I jogged through the lanes, following her voice, past the signs for cities and towns I'd never visited and families and fraternities I'd never been a part of. I found her with her arms crossed, waiting for me, smiling at her find, and I jogged up to meet her and say yes, indeed, there it is. I know this place.

Then renewed and sober, we dropped into the car again and drove on.

P.C.T. - PLEASE CALL THEM

David Hagerty

Unlike the national parks, Ansel Adams Wilderness doesn't draw a lot of tourists or day hikers. It's a long walk, six miles, up several thousand feet. The visitors there are committed woodsmen, backpackers, and fishermen who want to see places others can't. It's terrain for people who don't mind suffering. Yet when one of them appeared at my wilderness station saying he'd found a body, I doubted him. Rangers hear a lot of hysterical reports—everything from rabid beavers to Sasquatches—but my source wore the clothes and scruff of a die-hard, so I followed him to his discovery.

The shelter hid behind a stand of Lodgepole pines and several large granite slabs, a primitive camp above Thousand Island Lake. As I drew closer, I saw a lean-to tarp, under it, a young man wrapped in a sleeping bag. His hair was scraggly and long, his beard overgrown, his face deeply tanned and dirty. I protect thousands like him every summer, and typically they blaze through my stretch of woods so quickly I never get to check their permits, leaving only footprints and feces.

When I spoke, he didn't move. When I sniffed the air, he smelled unwell. When I shook his arm, it felt stiff. Definitely dead, but I couldn't tell from what. No blood or visible injuries on him—thank God. Although rangers enforce the law in the forest, we aren't adapted to homicide investigations. Yet that left a host of other causes: poison, parasite, allergy, heart attack, and lightning strike. His build suggested starvation, his dress exposure.

Aside from his body, my victim didn't leave many clues: two dehydrated meals in his bear can, some rain gear in his backpack, and a wilderness permit in his front pocket with the name Daniel Heymann.

I turned to my guide—a young fellow who spoke little English. He overused a toothy smile that he overused to disguise nervousness.

"You a thru-hiker?"

He smiled and gave an uncertain nod, making me uncertain if he understood.

"North or south?" I said.

"Up," he said and pointed north.

"Ever see him before?"

"No."

I took the guy's vitals and shooed him back to his tent, then clicked on my radio. Static replied. Most of the Sierra got no reception, and Thousand Island Lake was no exception. The nearest landline required six miles of hiking and double that in driving, which would take till dark. Three thousand feet above loomed Mount Ritter and Banner, which Ansel Adams made famous in his photos. From a few hikers, I'd heard about a sweet spot with a cell phone signal near the top. The climb would waste half a day if it failed but save as much if I found a window to the world.

The ravine heading out of the lakebed held pure volcanic rock, pocked and pointy. Higher up came a snow field-tinged pink with algae. We called it watermelon snow, but eating it would kill your appetite. It had softened in the midday sun so that several times I sank to my hips, and once I fell to all fours to stop myself from sliding. From there, I scrambled over boulders and scree devoid of life. I chose to call this adventure purposeful, but I took any excuse for an excursion. Nothing compared to the high of mountain air and a clear view.

Halfway up, I checked my radio and reached an intern at the main station who'd never heard of me or my mountain. When I requested a copter evac, she put me on hold, so I looked to the sun, which sat only a few ticks above setting. No way they'd send in a chopper this late. Even daylight landings are risky in the bush, and at night, pilots won't attempt it. They'd wait till the next morning. In the meantime, I needed to guard the body.

Before descending, I thought of phoning my wife, who hadn't heard from me in a week, but I saw only one bar on my cell phone. Instead, I glissaded down the snowbank, sliding like a carefree child while soaking my pants.

Two hours later, as alpenglow tinged the mountain, I found a flat slab near Daniel's body and unrolled my down bag. Camping so close to the dead did little for my sleep, and during the night, the wind picked up, sending the trees creaking against each other. I dreamt of Daniel's spirit struggling to escape—with me guarding the exit. Then I imagined strangulation and toxic mushrooms and awoke twisted in my sleep sack. By the time the helicopter arrived shortly after dawn, I felt like a bear coming out of hibernation: groggy, hungry, and irritable.

When the pilot and I lifted Daniel from one body bag to another, he weighed even less than I expected, no more than my Labrador. His fingers were so emaciated a silver ring slipped off one and fell into the dirt. Long-haul hikers get gaunt after months in the woods. It's near impossible for them to carry enough food to counterbalance the calories they burn. Except instant meals sat within his grasp. Why hadn't he eaten any?

Before zipping him away, I photographed his face with my cell phone—one of the few uses for one so far from civilization. Then, as the copter disappeared above me, I packed up his campsite and looked for clues, but his bag, pack, and tent all contained the minimal supplies you'd expect: water tablets, bug repellant, a map of the Sierra, well-worn boots.

Based on how thin and exposed Daniel looked, I pegged him for a thru-hiker on the Pacific Crest Trail, which bifurcated my wilderness. To complete all 2,600 miles, people had to cover twenty per day, starting in Mexico around March so they could hit the mountains as soon as the snow subsided, then tunnel through the forests of NorCal and Oregon to reach the Washington border before winter. They formed a mobile community, yet the guy who found him claimed not to have seen him prior, even though they had walked the same trails.

Then I looked below. The helicopter's turbulence had awoken everybody within a mile. Dozens of backpackers stood outside their tents, most still wearing their long underwear, watching where I stood. That gave me half an hour to interview people before they broke camp.

I didn't want to lose too much daylight, so I looked for the most grizzled visitors in hopes of tagging more PCTers. I found a trio of women warriors attired in the gear of their college crew team.

"How far you going?" I asked.

"All the way," said the sturdiest of the three in a flirtatious tone.

"So you've met some other thru-hikers?"

"Unfortunately," said a second, who had the same height and strength without the bulk. She stepped closer to speak in confidence, brushing my shoulder. "They're mostly weirdos."

"What about this guy?" I showed them Daniel's picture as they gathered close enough that my wife would disapprove.

"He was the worst," said the third, who looked pretty despite a grimy face. "The one time we tried to talk to him, he grunted."

"Totally antisocial," said the second. "Wouldn't even show us his map."

"When?"

"Muir Pass," said the first. "We all got trapped in that hut during a storm, but he just stared."

"Gave off a Donner Party vibe," said the second.

If those three couldn't draw him out, it said something about Daniel's personality. Loners liked it up here. You could go days without speaking to anyone. However, Daniel acted unusually antisocial.

I questioned a few other campers, but none claimed to know

the hermit of the hillside. Since even preliminary autopsy results would take a couple days, I had little to go on besides a name. In the backcountry, investigative methods are less scientific than organic. We used what nature gave us. I could spend the day interviewing every hiker who tramped through, or I could scale Banner again for outside sources.

The second time up proved both easier and chancier since the snow fields had frosted overnight—the kind of trek that usually required ice axes and crampons. I told myself I had good reason to risk hiking there alone, and that experience would guide me through, but I knew better. No one is immune to nature's hazards. Still, I enjoyed the sun's warmth and the way it glinted off the lake like God beams. At the prior sweet spot, my phone showed no bars, so I kept going, checking every quarter mile till just below the summit, I got a signal.

Daniel's permit listed a phone number, but directory assistance said the line had been disconnected. His address included a #3B after the street name, so I called the county recorders, who got me the number of his landlord.

"He moved out three months back," the guy said.

"He leave a forwarding address?"

"Some p.o. box in—."

The call dropped before I heard the name, so I angled the phone toward the sky until I got a signal again and called him back.

"Where?" I said.

"ILLINOIS," the guy said, annoyed.

"What about relatives? Anybody ever visit him?"

"I wouldn't know or care."

"You didn't like him?"

"He left without giving notice."

"So you don't have an emergency contact?"

He sighed and rustled some papers. "His mother. You want the number?"

I didn't, but I took it anyway. Notifying relatives is part of the job, but the worst part, especially in cases of fatal injury. About once a season, I had to make such a call, but usually for accidents: hikers and climbers who took a step too far. I couldn't think of any such explanation for Daniel's mom. Instead, I told her the news quick and cold.

"No, no, no, no, no," she said.

"Did Daniel have any medical conditions?"

"No, no, nothing."

"How about allergies?"

"No."

"Did he hike often?"

"Always. When he was a boy, I had to leash him to keep him from wandering off."

"So he had experience in the outdoors?"

"It's all he cared about. Two months ago, he quit his job so he could walk the West Coast."

"When did you last hear from him?"

"He sent one note midway. Said he was learning a lot about himself. That's how he put it, 'learning a lot about himself.' I wanted to scream, 'What do you need to know? I'll tell you.' But you can't scream in a letter, so I said, 'Come back when you find it.'"

She started crying, gasping, choking, which, combined with the static, made it tough to understand her. I got the locations of those drop boxes before she became incomprehensible, then I used bad reception as an excuse and promised to call back in a few days.

I've often said that P.C.T. really stands for Please Call Them. At least once a week, I got a message from some relative of a thru-hiker asking about their progress, as though I were a field biologist tracking animal migration. They didn't get how wild and remote the trail is and that it offered few spots with a landline to check in.

That high up, the Sierras appeared endless, wave upon wave of mountains and valleys limited only by human vision. The Thousand Islands for which the lake was named looked like mere dimples. Somewhere in that vastness, someone might know him, but I could spend the rest of the season searching for them. I'd eliminated most unnatural causes, but that left a lot unexplained. Instinct said to backtrack to where he'd been and talk to slower hikers he'd passed. If necessary, I could keep going to Lake Edison, the closest way station Daniel had given his mother, forty miles south along the P.C.T.

I thought again of calling my wife to let her know I'd be out of range, but I hadn't time to spare for conversation, so I returned to my wilderness station and packed a light bag. I left behind a tent and stove, opting to travel fast and light, despite the warning that Daniel's death provided.

The trip proved to be a snipe hunt, filled with bewildered backpackers—who added nothing but wanted me to recount the details of the death—until I met the hippie. He worked trail crew, clearing the way by rolling away boulders, sectioning fallen limbs, restoring rock walls and stair steps. His hair lay on his shoulders, limp and dirty, except for one thin braid that hung rigid by his face. He smelled of wood smoke and wild fish, and his body had leaned to sinewy muscles. Even his movements were economical, refined of everything non-essential.

"Dude didn't know how to live," he said.

"Which is?"

"Minute by minute. Like eating. No way you can get by on three squares out here. Your body needs hourly reinforcements, something to burn."

"You told him this?"

"Tried. He wouldn't listen. Too caught up in where he was going to see where he was."

"Because he started late?"

"Not that. What I think? Kept his mind busy." He nodded

to affirm his own wisdom. "Monkey mind. Can't stop moving. What I think? He didn't know how to stop."

I thanked him for his insights and jotted a few notes, mostly about where and when they'd met. This sage of the sticks offered more speculation than facts. I discounted his philosophy, which paraphrased the Doobie Brothers, but I accepted his insight about coming to a cliff on life's trek. Hadn't we all hit such an impasse? Lately, my back ached every morning, and my knees ached every night. How much longer could I keep the pace? Twenty summers I'd spent as a seasonal ranger, long enough to navigate the trails without a map, yet during my winters teaching biology to tech-obsessed teens, I daydreamed about returning to the woods.

The rest of the trek offered no enlightenment but a few good moments interspersed: a patch of Western Columbine in full bloom, their red dragon heads breathing fiery stamen; the song of a lonely pica; the lava stacks of Devils Postpile. I've always used the wilderness as my antidepressant, a check on self-absorption, a focus on the essentials: eating, sleeping, and moving. By the time I arrived at Lake Edison two days later, my mood had lifted.

John, aka Scree, ran a neat little operation, the world's most remote trailer park, selling supplies and soft beds to backpackers at inflated prices. He also held their mail, knowing that it would lure them in like hungry wolves to a fresh kill. I found him behind the bar that functioned as his office. He kept a spartan saloon, a mix and match of furniture handmade from desiccated wood and walls decorated with found objects (antlers, pelts, pine cones). He looked the same as always, chunky, out of shape, pale, the antithesis of the hikers he served.

"Look who the dog dragged in," he said.

We exchanged mountain gossip until I asked if he remembered my victim. He held my cell phone at arm's length as though it offended him. "After a month outside, they all look alike," he said. "What'd he do to draw your attention?"

"Died."

Without a word, Scree set up two shots of homemade whisky, then finished his in a swallow. "That we should all pass away in the woods."

"You think he stayed with you?"

"I don't keep records. You know the rules: first one with cash gets the bed."

"What about packages or letters?"

"If he picked it up, then it's gone. The U.S. government doesn't take kindly to me tracking their business."

"Wanna check?"

The way he snatched out the mail—at random, whatever caught his eye—I knew he'd given up alphabetizing. The patient and persistent travelers got their messages. The rest didn't care enough. Finally, after surveying nearly every parcel, he extracted an envelope. Red ink across the front read "return to sender," although the postmark dated a month old.

"Mail carriers refused to take it back," Scree said. "Seems the government wants more money after it's been opened."

"And you didn't have any?"

He shrugged and poured himself another drink.

A letter contained the loopy script of a woman and, behind that, a preliminary order from a divorce court. The note started: "Since you've run off, I have no other way to tell you…." The rest cataloged all the ways Daniel had failed to satisfy his wife's needs while tending to his own: too caught up in hunting, fishing, and camping to notice her discontentment. Halfway through, I quit reading. If I got a letter like that, I'd also want to walk a thousand miles away.

"So, how'd he die?" Scree asked.

I parsed all I'd learned about him: his sudden departure from home, his disinterest in society, his self-imposed starvation, his evasions of his mother. "I think he gave up."

"On his trip?"

"On other people."

Scree toasted me again, but the whiskey burned my throat even as the taste lingered on my tongue.

"So where to from here?" he said.

I thought of my wife, who hadn't seen me in two months or spoken to me in as many weeks. I possessed the same urge to wander as Daniel, except with less cause. Unlike his spouse, mine awaited my return. Only a woman at forty won't accept the same life she did at twenty. She indulged my wilderness wanderlust but deserved better than a three-quarters commitment.

"Home," I said.

COWLATERAL DAMAGE

J.C. Elkin

It was late September in Switzerland's Lauterbrunnen Valley, the lush pastures sparkling with frost-melt under the retreating shadows of the Alps. As we drove past chalets draped in geraniums, the sun warmed us like the mulled wine we would order in Mürren, a postcard hamlet halfway up the Schilthorn. There, where no cars were allowed, the Alpine breeze could transport an American tourist to the pages of *Heidi*, which was precisely what my aunt had in mind.

As with all pilgrimages, the journey was arduous, requiring a train and gondola ride that ran infrequently. And this particular day, the lowlands were rank with the scent of manure.

"Eww, Julia!" my husband teased our toddler, "Do you need to go potty?"

"Nooo," she protested, kicking his seat. "It's the cows. The cows are gassy."

Her big sister snickered, plugging her nose.

"Poor Julia," my aunt sympathized. "I believe you, even if I can't see them."

It was true. We hadn't passed any cattle yet, but the funk was strong. I was musing where they could be when a police cruiser with flashing lights came inching down the center of the road at 15 kilometers per hour. The officer slowed and waved our Honda Civic toward the shoulder.

"Oh, great," my husband said. "Construction! Now we'll never catch the train on time."

"Are you sure?" my aunt asked. "I didn't see any road work signs."

Again, she was right. There had been no signs, so we kept the motor running.

Our new car, purchased in '88, shortly before receiving military orders abroad, was roomy enough for a young family and small enough to be gentle on gas. Yet even with petrol at four times the stateside price, our tiny sedan had not proven as economical as we'd hoped. Built to American standards, it had presented unique challenges under the Swiss bureaucracy. In order to buy insurance, we'd had to invest $2,000 (US) to retrofit it with halogen headlights, beige blinkers, an official speedometer posting kilometers per hour larger than miles, and a hand-crafted muffler.

We were on a first-name basis with our *mécanicien* and the *agent d'assurances* who had helped us navigate the labyrinth of repairs and registration. Despite the headaches, though, the car had served us well—from Christmas tree shopping in the Jura to sledding in the Engadine and touring most of western Europe.

The officer strode to our vehicle, eyeing us like the foreigners we were.

"*Guete Morge. Könne Sie Schwitzerdütsch reede?*"

Neither of us spoke Swiss German.

"*Je parle français,* and I speak English," my husband replied.

"*Gut,*" the policeman replied. "Park on the verge of the road and break off your motor. The *Alpabzug* comes."

"What did he say?" I asked as he strolled away.

"Park on the shoulder and turn off the engine. I think we're going to see the *Dèsalpe,*" he said, his eyes bright with surprise. "At least that's what the French call it. I read about it in the weekend section of the newspaper. It's a festival to celebrate the milking cows' return from their high summer pastures. It's a big deal, a really momentous occasion. We're lucky!"

He pulled up to the grassy embankment and hopped out, camera at the ready. My aunt and I, holding the children's hands, stood behind the trunk for safety.

We heard the animals before we saw them, their great bells clanging a cacophony of copper, bronze, iron, and brass. First came two chestnut draft horses pulling a wagon with the farmer's family perched on parade. Then came children driving half a dozen white goats with wooden walking sticks. Everyone, young and old, wore traditional costumes: the beribboned girls in colorful dirndls with laced bodices and aprons, and the guys in dark suits embroidered with edelweiss and trimmed in red piping. They sported hunter- green fedoras or floppy peasant caps. Even the goats had red bows. Then came the cattle—Guernseys, buff-colored like our car and just as tall. On their heads were bouquets of pine boughs and wildflowers, and around their beefy necks, they wore huge bells corresponding to their productivity: the bigger the bell, the better the milker. The champion led the parade, weighted down by brass that hung to her knees.

"The poor cow," my aunt crooned, "having to carry all that weight."

She had a point. The bell must have weighed 30 pounds. Ironically, there was a move afoot a quarter-century later, in 2015, to outlaw even the traditional 12-pound bells when it was found that they damaged the animals' hearing, but farmers and the tourism bureau prevailed in that fight.

The lead cow trotted down the center dotted line with the rest of the herd fanning out behind her in a flying wedge formation. With too few herdsmen, the livestock owned the road, and they knew it. One of the leaders headed to the grassy shoulder in order to graze. Then another followed, and another, until soon they were overflowing the road.

"They're headed straight for us!" my husband said, his voice rising with alarm.

"Mooo," said the girls, making finger horns on their heads.

"Aren't they just the most adorable creatures you ever saw?" my aunt exclaimed.

"Girls, up here on the hill!" I called, reaching for them.

The herd picked up speed, and just as they reached our car, one bovine hip- checked another such that she belly-flopped onto the hood of our Honda, sliding forward with front hooves outstretched like a kid on a Slip-n-slide. She bellowed; the car groaned, and a loud *crunk* issued from the bumper as she slid over the hood and eased off the fender with surprising grace. It was over in five seconds. Five dumbfounded seconds, and not a photo to show for it. Nothing but a crumpled hood slimed with milk and drool, and a side- view mirror hanging limp from its wire—another $2,000 in repairs.

"The poor cow," my aunt said.

"My poor car!" my husband said.

"My God!" I said. "We were lucky, all right. Lucky we weren't killed."

When we returned to town later that afternoon to file an official report, we learned that ours was one of five vehicles damaged by the herd that day, for which the farmer's insurance company, Winterthur (motto: *Acting Responsibly*), had to settle claims. We received compensation only when our Winterthur agent, a personal friend, intervened on our behalf, the farmer claiming that the spectators in their parked cars were at fault.

We made it to Mürren that day to nurse our warm drinks on a terrace overlooking the Jungfrau. And, of course, we bought a cowbell to commemorate the occasion. We have it still and ring it to commemorate momentous occasions like graduations, weddings, and car accidents.

GOODBYE TO DALLAS

Ann Howells

Every good story begins
with someone either coming or going.
I'm going
past the gym where hamsters run on little wheels,
burger joint where a long line awaits
the drive-thru,
and the stadium where our local team gears up
for another losing season.

Coffee shop on every corner;
people staring at little blue screens. It's progress.
Another glass building pops from the ground –
a humongous crystal
formed by developers' heat and politicians' pressure.
Traffic arteries harden –
driving is blood sport here – SUVs and big-rigs
roll over my reflection on the windshield.

The road spools out, red dotted line of taillights.
Traffic flows I-35 –
tip of South America all the way to Prudhoe Bay.
Green road signs give mileage
to Beaumont, El Paso, Amarillo.
I teeter on the edge of civilization – almost out of Texas.

SAN ANTONIO ON MY BIRTHDAY

Ann Howells

From seven stories up:
boats seem fantasy floats in a Rose Parade,
bloom with tourists in flowered shirts.
And down here, on the riverwalk,
riffs of mariachi music –
trumpet, guitarron, violin – carry
on intermittent breezes.
But I am swaddled in the music
of language: Spanish, Spanglish, English,
even tourists rolling their Rs.
I buy a small clay pot –
three legs and head of a goat –
two *Dia de los Muertes* figures –
bull and bullfighter.
Whiffs of grilled fajitas, chiles,
and sweet cinnamon scent of sopapillas
draw me into a tiny restaurant –
salty-lime taste of a margarita
makes me linger, relax,
watch tourists and natives mingle,
lost in the music of a language
I cannot even speak.

THE MIDDLE OF CATSKILL-NOWHERE

Katie Baker

We drive through a world made white by high vaporous mist and fog that hang atop the hills like a meringue. It switches between rain and snow all morning, and the further east we drive, the heavier the crust of ice and snow becomes at the edge of the road. The four-lane remains deserted. We pass road signs posted deep in gullies that say things like, "Welcome to the Western Catskills." The abandoned summer camps with their over-grown ghost cabins look anything but welcoming.

Like most of rural New York, poverty clings to the soil at the bottom of these gullies, and the detritus of their former jobs sit smoldering and rotting just a few miles down the road.

I don't think much of it, though. You don't think of it much when you grow up around it.

My boyfriend and I talk of other more profound things — the real crux of a solution for humanity: whether Twitter was, in fact, an over-blown employer and if they'll fall apart without all those employees. I mean, it's the heart of the issue for the shanty-dwellers in the depths of the hollers, right?

I'm avoiding thinking of a lot today, like are we headed to a Stewart Shops in the middle of Catskill-nowhere to be murdered? Or will we buy a Subaru Forester from a guy? Should I have given up my Saturday to do this or stayed home to work on my writing? I don't think about them because my boyfriend and I so seldomly get to talk to each other on our road trips. Usually, we're on a motorcycle.

"Oh, crap!" my boyfriend says mid-sentence when we're only a half hour away from the middle of Catskill-nowhere.

"What?" I sit straighter in my seat, thinking something's wrong with my car.

"I forgot the plates— I was gonna bring my plates to put on just to get us home — hopefully— without being stopped."

"Oh... Well— what do we do now?"

My boyfriend shrugs, grimacing. "Hope he lets us take it with the plates, and we'll mail them back."

"Do you think he will?"

"I mean, some people do— It just depends on the guy, I guess."

A moment of silence passes.

"Oh, crap!" repeats my boyfriend.

"What?!"

"I forgot the bill of sale form, too!"

"Seriously?"

"Maybe the Stewart Shops has a printer..."

About a half hour later, we pull into a much-diminished Stewart Shops parking lot. Great curls of ice and snow eat up half the parking spaces; they remind me of butter shaved from the block. The rain/snow has started again, and we race inside to find a bathroom. We predictably forget to ask about a printer and the bill of sale form. Instead, we waste time rearranging my car in the parking lot.

We just get it situated when I see a dark gray Forester pull around and back into the space beside the air pump.

"Is that them?" I nod toward the Forester. A tall man dressed in white T-shirt and black sweatpants emerges from one side, and a teenage boy pops from the other.

"Looks like it." A hint of excitement creeps into my boyfriend's voice. "It doesn't look like anyone else drove here with them..." My boyfriend squints at the pair again. "That doesn't seem promising."

It doesn't look like they're even prepared for this to be a long transaction; neither wears a coat. The man's T-shirt (his name is Buck) stretches over a ripe-round belly, and it looks like he's wearing slippers. The boy has on a hoody but is wearing shorts, and his legs look sunburnt already in the damp cold.

"You___?" says Buck as we approach.

"Yeah." My boyfriend shakes his hand from around the bundle of coveralls he carries trapped beneath his elbow.

"There she is—" Buck motions toward the idling Forester. The door sits open, collecting plops of raindrops and snow chunks— a fat wad of keys swings from the ignition.

My gut sinks at the sight of those keys— like the Forester isn't prepared for existence without Buck.

"Were you not expecting me to take it home today?" my boyfriend asks.

"Yeah, well— you know— I just get effed around by these dipshits who get here and wanna offer 4 for it— like, no man. I know what it's worth. I'm already selling it at a loss."

"Yeah— I noticed you posted it before. I messaged you about it last year, and you never got back to me." My boyfriend struggles into his coveralls as he talks.

"Well, that's it, man. I was getting fucked over by all these smart asses— and finally, I just said, 'Nah, I'll just keep it. If you ain't going my price, I'll just keep it.'"

"Why are you selling it, if you don't mind my asking?" my boyfriend speaks from the ground where he's inspecting the undercarriage.

"So, like, I bought it for my wife, right? But she don't drive stick, and I don't think she wants to learn. Like, she keeps saying, 'I will. I will,' but then she don't. And this is like my fourth vehicle. Like I got too many fucking cars."

Buck talks fast; his facts and family tidbits trip over each other on their way out, and his conjunctions all seem to be joined by "fuck." But he rounds the car with my boyfriend and points out the dents and bruises. He says the tires are all seasons, but they have the least aggressive tread I've ever seen on all seasons. He says it's been a good car; he just can't justify keeping it if his wife won't learn manual.

The initial inspection done, Buck says, "You can test drive it if you want. We can jump in the back."

"So if I'm sold on it, you just—like—want me to drive you home?" Buck's brows flex. "Oh yeah, man. No problem. No problem. We could do that."

We begin to pile in the car. Buck lets my boyfriend put his coveralls in the trunk since it's becoming apparent he's buying the vehicle. Just as we're getting situated, my boyfriend says: "Oh, yeah, the money." He trots across the parking lot to my car, leaving me completely alone with Buck and his son. My mind flashes to all the True Crime tales of internet transaction predators, and I try to keep my heart rate steady.

I make inane remarks about the weather to distract myself from being alone with strangers, but I feel a lot better when my boyfriend climbs into the driver's seat beside me. When we start, though, I can't shake the unease that situation gave me.

We drive up through a brightening landscape. The sun struggles to appear through the high, white haze, and the rain/snow shower tapers to a fine mist. We climb past well-kept houses and shacks, some abandoned properties with caved-in rooves, and a few farms with far-away silos. Buck directs us where to turn and gives us a brief history of the car as he knows it. An old guy owned it before him. He did some work for this guy, and he saw the Forester was a manual, and he just had to have it.

"He babied it, man— I baby it. Like, I'm too old for that race car driver shit. I gotta take care of my vehicles."

"What is it you do?" my boyfriend asks. "You said you did work for the guy. What kind of work?"

"I'm a contractor."

"What kind of contracting?"

"Oh, everything— Everything except electrical." Buck laughs.

"Why not electrical?"

"I don't like getting shocked! Haha! Plus, all my friends are fucking electricians. Like I need someone for a job, I just call Steve, you know."

"Yeah. Yeah."

We twist and turn further into the gullies between the mountains. The contrast between the houses grows vaster the further into the heart of the tall, spindly trees that we drive. We pass one that looks like a millionaire CEO threw it up yesterday, and then the next one is practically made of clapboard with dogs churning up the yard behind a rusted chainlink fence.

My boyfriend explains the problem with the bill of sale and the license plates. Buck assures us the plates aren't a problem, but the bill of sale may be trickier. They have a printer at home, but he doesn't know how to use it. His son says he's sure his sister knows how to use it.

The roads narrow as we get closer to his house, and the low-fuel light dings on just after the final turn.

"Oh yeah, you'll make it back on that," says Buck. "It's only like 13 miles from my house to the Stewart Shops."

My feeling of unease makes me shift in my seat.

We squeeze our way into a drive, switching back as we turn. A homemade plankboard sign hangs from a tree trunk. Usually, in this setting, these signs say, "No trespassing" or "Fuck Joe Biden." This one says, "Black Lives Matter." I chuckle. It's like we've left rural New York and have teleported to Vermont.

We pull to a stop at the crest of the lane; Buck's driveway dips down toward his house. The road that continues past is seasonal use, and what we can see of it was plowed by Buck with the work truck sitting at the top of his drive. A homemade metalwork peace sign hangs from the tree at the fork, and Buck's tiny house sits nestled against the hillside. His yard is full of tools, equipment, and kids' toys, and I wonder that he owns a printer.

We get out and wait in his driveway for him to retrieve the title, check the printer, and bring back a bag to clean the rest of his stuff from the consoles. It begins to snow again as we wait—fluffy, wet flakes cascade toward us through the tree trunks. From the top of the drive, I look out over the gully, over the trailer's roof below, and even though there's not much of a view, the place feels open and bright. This probably changes in summer. The sun struggles through the haze again— just a pale ball of bleached yellow. The chunky snowflakes splash against my cheeks and catch in my eyelashes.

Buck stays gone for a long time. A very long time.

My feet start to go numb. I didn't wear thick enough socks to stand still on cold, wet ground for this long. I stomp around to stay moving and study the star- shaped imprint left by the sole of my boot. My boyfriend stalks around the car, and we both try hard not to look toward the house often.

Finally, we crawl back into the Forester, too cold to stand in the mud. "Maybe they can't get the printer working," my boyfriend says.

"Maybe..." but the peace of the snow shower has left me. Now, I can only think of how rural and secluded this place is— the last house, off the final turn, on a hillside above I-don't-remember-where.

"It feels weird sitting in his car," I say. "Like— you haven't given him the money yet."

Suddenly, Buck appears in the doorway. He struggles up the steep drive carrying a piece of paper, a child's multichoice pen, and a cigarette.

My boyfriend and I step back out into the snow shower.

"Listen, man," Buck says around the unlit cigarette. "I got bad news about the plates. She doesn't want me to send you with 'em. You know— like, the car's in her name, and she's worried about the insurance and registration and all that— like, I'm real sorry, man... You think you'll be able to get back without plates?"

My boyfriend's expression flexes, and I know it's his we-gotta-do-what-we-gotta- do look. "I mean, I'd prefer not to, but we should be okay with the bill of sale. We shouldn't get a ticket if I explain."

"Well, that's the other thing— the bill of sale." Buck waves the now limp and splotchy piece of paper. "This is all we could get to print off." He holds it up, and I see more wet blossoms on the nearly blank sheet.

"Well, I do need that— I can't get it registered without the bill of sale."

"Oh, I know. I know. We're gonna get one and get it filled out. I'm gonna put it priority mail first thing Monday."

Ironically, his wife won't trust us with her plates, but now we need to trust her husband with the bill of sale.

"You should take a picture of the plates," Buck says. "And I'll write you up something— just in case you get stopped. I gotta get the title from her. She's signing it now."

He stomps back down the driveway, the unlit cigarette hanging from his mouth and the computer paper disintegrating in his fist. I wonder how long he'll be gone this time and climb back into the Forester.

Mercifully, we only wait about a minute. Buck returns with an envelope, notebook, and the same pen. This time I stay in the car. By now, the car belongs to my boyfriend (pretty much), and my feet feel like blocks of ice.

"I just need your address," says Buck, again from around the unlit cigarette.

My boyfriend tries two different color inks from the multichoice pen. Finally, one works. Buck hands him the half-ripped envelope. "That's the title and what I've written out in place of the bill of sale."

My boyfriend inspects both.

"And I'll mail everything you need for registration on Monday."

"Okay..." my boyfriend nods and reaches into his Carhart pocket for his envelope full of hundreds. He hands this to Buck.

"It's a good car, you know," Buck says, taking the money. "It'll be a good ride for you." He steps away a foot or two and pulls a lighter from his pocket instead of counting the money. He uses the envelope stuffed with hundred-dollar bills to shield the flame from the wind. I watch the spark catch twice centimeters from the bills before his cigarette lights.

Visions of burning C-notes float through my mind.

Cigarette glowing merrily, Bucks peels back the edge of the envelope and counts the straps. His lips turn up ever so slightly around his smoke, and he raises his hand toward my boyfriend.

They shake.

"Pleasure doing business with you, man," Buck says. "I'll keep you updated on the paperwork."

"I appreciate it."

"Let me know if you get stopped." Buck's eyes crinkle when he chuckles.

"Sure thing, man." My boyfriend settles into the driver's seat, and Buck disappears down his muddy driveway one last time.

What I feel backing down the lane is more than just elation at having bought a car— I feel relief. For some reason, that pressure I felt about internet killers and shady people had grown oppressive looking down at the mud and clutter surrounding Buck's house. He seemed all right, but I was overjoyed, quite honestly, to be away from him.

It doesn't even bother me that now I must drive three hours west stuck to my boyfriend's bumper— hoping we don't get pulled over. These are the small prices I pay for adventure.

THE NATIONAL ROAD

Tim Morris

Where are you going this summer? people asked in the spring of 2022. To see my son in Virginia, I replied, but then I'm going to drive back along the National Road. Where to? they followed up. Nowhere, I said. I'm not taking it to get anywhere. I want to see the National Road itself.

When you look at the National Road route on a map today, you're struck by the aimlessness of it. Its official endpoints are Vandalia, Illinois, and Cumberland, Maryland—not places many people want to get to or from anymore. The Road lurches northwest out of Cumberland across a depopulated corner of Pennsylvania, nips across West Virginia, and then plows into the prairie. Its convenience as a route from Columbus to Indianapolis is most obvious, explaining why I-70 closely parallels it there today.

But back in its heyday, the early-mid-19th century, the National Road was a vital corridor. Cumberland was as far up the Potomac as one could effectively navigate. The Pennsylvania portion of the Road was the most efficient cut across the shortest reach of the Appalachians. Wheeling gave the Road a Virginia and Ohio River port (long before West Virginia seceded). The westward stretch connected (at the time) three state capitals: Columbus, Indianapolis, and Vandalia.

I don't entirely know what I expected to find. I mused vaguely that hewing to each twist and turn of the National Road would prompt synesthetic images of primeval stagecoach journeys or even lower-tech ramblings from the past. I wanted to take a dynamic dip into history—to imagine what it was like to ride the Road, to bounce along it in a stagecoach, to drive flocks of sheep on it to market. I would sojourn a while in the steps of long-ago pilgrims, stripping away the accretions of modern development—and, of course, this all turned out to be complete nonsense. I might as well have stayed home in bed, read books about the Old Pike, and daydreamed about the picaresque days of yore.

———— ✦ ————

In any case, historic roads, as tourist attractions, are by definition nothing like what they used to be. Not an inch of the road you take will be what people traveled even a century before. Most of it will barely resemble what you drove all that way to drive.

In her wonderful book *The Ruins Lesson*, Susan Stewart observes that even ruins must be continually maintained. When you visit the Baths of Caracalla, you brush past the ghosts of long-ago Roman bathers, and also those of slightly less-long-ago medieval and Romantics and archeologists and curators who all brought something—in many cases took away something— to produce the half-wild grandeur that the Baths display now, evoking what we can only imagine they were, to begin with.

With roads, Roman or otherwise, the transformation is total. Even to be perceptible amid the forces that constantly threaten to close over it, a road must be constantly re-hewn out of its surroundings. Leave a road not taken too long, and it will not only lie in leaves no step had trodden black; it will disappear entirely underneath brush and saplings and successor forests. If you can drive (or ride on horseback or bicycle, or for that matter walk) that road, it must be continually repaved and often re-graded and re-metaled.

Along the National Road, this reworking has meant replacement not just of surfaces but of the whole road structure. Especially between towns where the old route still follows the originally surveyed path from Cumberland to Vandalia, the successor roads—US-40, I-70—rarely follow the original cuts. Over its two centuries, the Road has been widened, deepened, straightened, moved—rationalized to conform to the best practices of new generations.

The resulting pattern resembles the sinuous rewinding of ancient river channels. A typical stretch of National Road, let's say in Ohio, might consist of several different parallel streams. I-70 attracts most of the traffic and is the least cognizant of its environment. The wide lanes and medians of the Interstate float on their imperceptible supporting tissue of bridges and overpasses. Here and there, a frontage road escorts them; entrances and exits carry the inflow and overflow. I-70 attracts almost all the traffic. Alongside—sometimes miles away, sometimes hemming I-70 so close that it doubles across and back, under and over the Interstate, at times subsumed altogether into the big road—runs US-40. Then, at intervals, a road called "Old 40," or just "National Pike," will diverge from the US highway to throw 40 itself—which might otherwise look now like a minor backroad—into relief as a great no-nonsense barreler—through from a century past.

"Old 40" often leads into a village where it becomes Main Street. The buildings on Main Street sometimes hug it close, as in Centerville, showing that they were once homes and inns on the "Old Pike." But sometimes, it's clear that Main Street itself is a widened alternative to the original route, which lingers on as old Old 40, running a block or two away, a parallel, barely trafficked street. Often, these old Olds dead-end, vestiges of the National Road that trail off or vanish into the grid of the town. Sometimes, the Old Pike becomes an oxbow, connecting to Main Street at neither end, accessible only from a tortuous turnoff. But even those oxbows must still be graded and paved and pothole-patched, winter after winter if they're to stay in the street grid at all. Under their motley surfaces, they come as close as you can get, by car or ultimately only on foot, to the routes so many stagecoaches plunged along in the mid-19th century. They are not the genuine Road anymore. That Road, temporary from the get-go, now lies inaccessible under their living surface. They persist as neglected but still viable paths. People still live on them; shops struggle to make a go of it even as the great rivers of commerce pass them by—in their seclusion on cutoffs from half-abandoned highways that nip at the flanks of frenetic Interstates.

————— ✦ —————

I started my tour after a much more functional drive east from Texas, on a venerable enough stretch of the Road in Hancock, Maryland, that features a toll house and a gravel pullout where you can park and walk around, though the building was inaccessible.

Inaccessible buildings are a big part of traveling the National Road. So is solitude. As I tramped the overgrown lawn at the Hancock toll house, I saw another car pull onto the gravel. It waited a few beats; nobody got out; it drove off. Those were my first five minutes on the Road, and that was the closest I got to having a fellow tourist anywhere I stopped. For the next three days, I would have the National Road to myself—not in the sense that there was no other traffic (though at times there was little enough of that), but in the sense that absolutely nobody else wanted to see the things I had come to see.

I slept fitfully outside of Cumberland, in a motel set absurdly up on the very top of a conelike hill, peering down at a cemetery in a valley below. I had allowed two-and-a-half days to drive to Vandalia—weirdly, both too much and too little time. Back home in Texas, I had spent weeks with Karl Raitz's magisterial *A Guide to the National Road* (1996), making detailed notecards on just where to turn off to see what remarkable vestige of the Pike. I zoomed in on Google Maps until my laptop screen showed quirks of the route displayed in lovingly enormous scale—only to find in practice that I shot past them at 60 miles an hour, an 18-wheeler on my tail.

On US-40 west of Frostburg, big trucks flashed by ten or fifteen miles faster than I was going. The roles reversed as I passed an Amish horse and carriage. I think that's the way to do this. If I could only ride a horse the length of the old Road. Or walk. Those would be 19th-century ways of seeing it. Though if I tried either, I would probably be struck and killed before even getting to Pennsylvania.

I stopped for reflection at Casselman River Bridge State Park—once again, the only person that morning who did so. By contrast to the modest effort in Clarysville, the Casselman Bridge is massive, a stone arch that in its day—its day being 1813—was among the engineering wonders of North America. The facing of the bridge dates from 1911, and the surface is much newer, almost unworn. Casselman Bridge was closed to car traffic long ago, though it looks in far better shape than the rusty structure that carries US-40 along beside it.

The Casselman Bridge survives by dint of sheer weight. It looks good for another 200 years. As I went back toward my car, it occurred to me that I was able to walk the Casselman Bridge because, in 1813, its builders messed up. They designed and constructed a bridge 40 or 50 times sturdier than it needed to be, a bridge that, unless deliberately detonated—and not even that would be easy—would long outlast the roadway it carried and even the concept of the National Road itself: a monument to the overpitched ambitions of its architects.

———— ✦ ————

As the Road angled northwest into Pennsylvania, the blur gathered, and the day collapsed into a palimpsest of impressions. I had to give up on my plan of consulting my notecards every few miles and meticulously following the surviving vestiges of older road cuts as they peeled away from modern US- 40. My 1996 guidebook, just 26 years later, reads like fiction now: businesses gone, landmarks destroyed, old cutoffs vanished. US-40 up through the western Pennsylvania woods is narrow, fast, and stressful.

Suddenly, a huge red sign loomed: DANGEROUS MOUNTAIN. Trucks were commanded to go at 10mph, in their lowest gear, and stop regularly at the mouths of runaway ramps. I was in a Honda Fit, but the grade was nearly impossible, even for my featherweight vehicle. Some behemoth had grabbed the Earth's surface by the scruff and pulled it vertically in order to shake anything unattached into a tremendous dustpan. After barely getting uphill, I had to choose, on the descent, between stressing the motor in a dangerously low gear or riding the brake all the way down lest I fly off the hillside into the ether.

And apparently, this hilarious test of alacrity was always a feature of the National Road, from its beginnings "awfully precipitous, and darkly umbrageous," as a traveler wrote in 1819. Stagecoaches used to thunder down, lethally overloading their horses' knees. In the early automotive days, drivers would hire professionals to take their cars down Dangerous Mountain. Or so I learn now, returning to my guidebook. I should have taken better notes.

Suddenly, I was in Ohio, and it seemed I had seen nothing at all. I redoubled my efforts to delve into old village street grids and fulfill my mission as a National Road tourist. The small towns of Ohio seemed to alert one another to gather their wits and resist my intrusion. Old Washington, Cambridge, New Concord – one village after another drew me into its streets and flung me out the other side without much sense of where the National Road cut across them. You would think that grids are grids and that if you stray, a strict algorithm of repeated turns should take you back to the road you came in on. Not so. I kept taking roads called "Eleventh Street," which seemed sure bets to cross Elm or Cherry and provide a way back to Tenth and Ninth Streets, but no; Eleventh Street would morph immediately into a narrow country lane, channeled by fence lines and steep ditches, to hurtle me twenty miles out of town before providing any shoulder to turn from and retrace my steps.

For my one night in Ohio, I'd picked a motel outside of Zanesville, a stop to represent the car culture that replaced stagecoach life on the National Road. Bilious wall paint, dingy ceiling tile, green bathroom with a cunning ventilator set between glass bricks, and though No Smoking, my room was undeniably one where people had smoked steadily for decades and left behind an aura that could never be stripped away. But somehow, I slept better in that room than in any of the generic new motels in other states. The motel had aged organically, mellowing in tobacco smoke, and the air that snuck in through the vent was a welcome contrast to climate control.

———— ✦ ————

From my stack of notecards, I picked a place called Gratiot to turn off and explore. Gratiot, Ohio, is a village of 200 with its own post office. The old Pike is Main Street; there's a secondary street called South Alley. At one end of town, a stout stone bridge carries the roadway on its back so the cutoff can rejoin US-40 a mile further along. In June 2022, Gratiot had a land-that-time-forgot, middle-American scrubbedness under an aquamarine sky. Utility poles, American flags, and generous front lawns (unflanked by sidewalks) descend onto the asphalt of Main Street. 180 years ago, this was the busiest road in the United States. Today, as so often along the Road, I didn't see a soul.

Then, through Amsterdam and Etna—all the placenames of Europe seem shaken up in a box and dumped onto Ohio—on my way to Columbus. Amsterdam is a typical Pike village, up on a rise above US-40: the current highway was later cut through a hill that the older National Road had climbed. The new route is more direct and wider; in Amsterdam, the houses huddle so close to the roadbed that no widening could occur. By chance, the surface of the Old Pike in Amsterdam had been repaved only days before. It glistened in the sunlight, a deep, satisfying blacktop above the bleached, patchy bed of 40 below. One of the oldest stretches of road I drove on during my trip was also the newest.

———— ✦ ————

I paused at the art museum in Richmond, Indiana: a gem of a place that holds a priceless large-scale self-portrait of William Merritt Chase. Most people outside the Midwest do not even know there is a Richmond, Indiana. But like many of the other cities in the region, its past opulence has left a distillation of fine art behind, a high-water mark of a collecting culture fueled by long-ago industrialization (at one point, much of the recorded music in America was produced in Richmond).

The next morning was my last on the Road. I had spent far more time thinking about this trip than carrying it out—the reverse of my usual summer travel, where I get off a plane in Stockholm or somewhere knowing almost nothing about the place except the names of the fictional detective inspectors who solve murders there. US-40 follows the old National Road route through Indianapolis as Washington Street, though you would be hard-pressed to identify many survivors of the old Pike in the city. The same is true in Terre Haute, where 40 joins the street grid, passing a huge sign proclaiming the city as the Home of Clabber Girl Baking Powder.

In Illinois, I met more frustration; despite my sense that the National Road is better marked there as a scenic highway, its historic cutoffs are better tended than in other states. The expository infrastructure of US-40 in Illinois is excellent, but the roadbed becomes a washboard. Driving the highway was like hitting a speed bump every second and a half, and when I slowed to take them every two seconds, the benefit was minimal, and the annoyance to the huge pickup trucks behind me was all but palpable. I opted for I-70 as far as Bluff City, Illinois, and then risked my tires on the last few corrugated miles.

My trip ended at the Vandalia State House, the capitol building of Illinois, back when Abraham Lincoln was an unfledged legislator. And what had I learned? That Heraclitus, if he'd owned a car, might have remarked that you never drive on the same road twice. Something gets built, something gets torn down, something crumbles, something tunnels below the metal. Travelers, like molecules of water, wash away at the roads they drive, taking bits away, shedding bits they bring. I exchange words, as few as possible, but still the currency of language, with innkeepers, waitstaff, and guys who sit outside gas stations and complain about the weather. Their language changes mine and mine theirs, infinitesimally, without perception on anyone's part.

Every itinerary everyone takes is like a snowflake or a thumbprint, in outline like the routes of thousands of others but irreducibly its own way. So, while one can set out to see a road the way one can the Brooklyn Bridge or the battlefield at Gettysburg, the sheer aliveness of the Road as a thing makes it an irreproducible monument, something you can never know entirely or ever show to others. And if you did, they would not care a whit.

DON'T BLINK OR YOU'LL MISS IT

Mary Kreienkamp

Sixty years ago, my uncle, the fighter pilot, took my father for a ride in his single-engine Cessna. It was the first and last time my dad set foot on a plane. "Your father is against flying," my mother would explain to my brother and me as if it were a deeply held moral conviction. But while Dad was opposed to airplanes, he fully supported matching their times on the road. After decades as a fireman, he had become accustomed to the speed that only sirens can provide.

To Dad, speed was essential "to get things done." It was imperative "to get things done" as early as possible in order to move on to the next things that needed to get done. This philosophy drove every aspect of his life, including family vacations. Thanks to Dad, I grew up thinking it was normal for vacations to begin at 3 a.m. Then again, I also grew up thinking aftershave was called "panther piss" until I tried to purchase it at the Macy's counter for Father's Day.

Under the hazy suburban starlight, Dad would fill our black Ford station wagon with the gear we'd need to set a land speed record: the tent we'd pitch each night by the glow of a bug-bombarded lantern and drop each morning before dawn, the coolers of meals Mom had prepared in advance to minimize pesky interruptions like eating, the Coleman stove over which she'd warm our dinners in darkness. As we pealed from our driveway onto the still sleeping street, Dad would glance in the rearview mirror and utter the words that began every family vacation, "Let's see how quickly we can get back."

While my father's pre-eminent goal was the timely completion of our trip, my mother's was our survival. She would try valiantly to slow her husband down. "Look!" her arm would shoot toward the shoulder of the highway. "State trooper has that guy pulled over!"

"Poor son of a bitch," Dad would reply, and floor it past the distracted officer.

But speed wasn't the only weapon in Dad's arsenal. The man stopped for nothing.

As we pulled into Hershey, Pennsylvania, expecting to immerse ourselves in chocolate goodness, he leaned over the steering wheel and gazed at the streetlights in the shape of Hershey's Kisses. "See those chocolate things?" he asked.

"Yeah," my brother and I answered.

"OK, that's Hershey then," Dad announced, signaling the end to our visit.

Colonial Williamsburg proved even more elusive. As we crossed an intersection, Dad slowed the car and urged, "Look down that street and tell me what you see."

I leaned forward and squinted past him. In the distance, bonnet-topped women, arms entwined in baskets, welcomed visitors into wood-paneled two-story homes. "I see old houses and people in costumes."

"Ok, seen enough?" Dad asked, "There's someone behind me."

With that, he hit the gas with such force that I tumbled backward, choking on my answer.

"Don't blink or you'll miss it," my mom mumbled from the back seat, and I wasn't quite sure if it was sarcasm or a helpful tip.

Our 1981 trip to Florida began as usual, then: in the dark. By the time the summer sun made its eye-watering appearance, we had followed the orange-highlighted TripTik route across the Ohio River into Paducah, Kentucky. I flipped ahead in the guide to see Dad's plans: St. Augustine, Daytona Beach, Silver Springs, Cypress Gardens, Tampa/St. Pete, Kennedy Space Center. From a kid's perspective, there was one glaring omission. "Dad, can we go to Disney World?"

"No time," came his automatic reply.

That seemed an easy problem to solve.

"Can we go to Disney World instead of Silver Springs?"

"Silver Springs has glass-bottom boats!" Dad exclaimed as if that could compete with the Happiest Place on Earth.

"How about Cypress Gardens?" I tried again.

"That's where the Esther Williams movies were filmed!" he replied incredulously as if I should not only know who she was but also recognize her greatness.

Clearly, this would require more work.

Eleven hours and twenty mentions of Disney World later, we arrived in St. Augustine, fifteen minutes before the closing of the Spanish fort. "Perfect timing!" Dad beamed.

We unfolded ourselves from the car, shook the blood clots from our legs, and hurriedly hobbled around the interior courtyard of the fort, extending our necks at each gaping doorway like a family of chickens on speed. We saw nothing but darkness beyond those doorways, but at least it was 300-year-old darkness.

Our courtyard lap completed, we found ourselves with sweat stinging our eyes and shirts sticking to our skin. It was Florida's hottest week in a decade, and, for once, we were relieved to return to the air-conditioned car. As we sped towards Daytona, my mother uttered the question that began a revolution, "Dad, don't you think it's too hot to camp?"

To our left, white sands and azure seas peaked from between beachfront condos, but the vision on our right riveted our attention: the yellow flashing arrow, more bulbs burnt out than blinking, screaming "All Rooms $14.99." Our eyes followed the arrow to a flat-roofed, one-story motel whose peculiar shade of pink I've since learned to call "dirty." Dad swung into the lot, secured a room key from the motel office, and ushered us into a wonderland of air conditioning and indoor plumbing, complete with toilet, sink, AND shower! "Just like home!" I marveled. The double beds were equipped with a miracle of modern science called Magic Fingers, which could be ours for fifteen minutes for a mere quarter. We didn't spend that quarter, but we *could have*. I hadn't known such luxury could be bought for $14.99 a night, or, according to the sign in the office window, $3.99 an hour.

My mother, I noticed, was not sharing my glee. She opened our cooler, retrieved the hamburger patties she had shaped before our trip, and fretfully plugged in our electric skillet. "*This is against the rules*," she whispered toward the sprinkler above her. As she dropped the patties onto the skillet, her husband, the fireman, leaped into action. With each sizzle, he cranked up the A/C another notch and squeezed the wet towel he had molded around the sprinkler. By the time the meat had browned, I was shivering under covers with no need for Magic Fingers, and Mom's face read, "We will discuss this later."

Mom slid the finished burgers onto thick slices of homemade bread, but the poor patties were no match for the frigid room. "A little cool," my dad commented as he bit into his burger, and my mother's look morphed to "Never again."

"You know what would be really cool?" I said, playing off my dad's ill-conceived remark, "Disney World."

The next day was a blur of scenery flashing by our car windows, but as dusk approached, it was clear the "discussion" had taken place. "Dad, don't you think it's time to stop for dinner?" my mom inquired, although we knew it was actually a statement and not a question. We were sitting at a stoplight, facing a billboard advertising "Morrison's All-You-Can-Eat Buffet: $2.99/person". They had my dad at "All-You-Can-Eat," but $2.99 made gluttony seem like frugality.

Maybe angels didn't sing as Dad entered Morrison's, but it was clear he had found his heaven on earth. As we drove into any Southeastern city from that day forward, he'd pull to the curb by the first telephone booth he saw. "Now!" he'd excitedly command, and I'd jump out, leaf through the White Pages, and write down the addresses of all the Morrison's in town.

We'd made our way through many of Florida's finest Morrison's—but not Disney World—when we found ourselves in a St. Petersburg motel, having completed a deep-sea fishing excursion where my mother and brother turned green. Our next destination was Kennedy Space Center, and Dad announced we'd depart at 3 a.m. because it was on the other side of the state.

5:30 a.m. found us detained in a small lot outside the towering Kennedy Space Center gate, with Security peering into our car to see who was attempting a pre-dawn entry. After waiting an hour for the gate to open, and another two for the Visitor's Center, we secured the first tour of the day. As we walked back to our car, Dad tried to turn the morning's experience into a teaching moment, "When you get the first tour, you have the rest of the day to get things done."

"Like go to Disney World?" I asked.

But to our dismay, we were going nowhere. During our pre-dawn arrival, we hadn't turned off our lights. After four hours waiting for AAA, I made my way to a nearby bench, next to a white-haired lady whose eyes smiled at me over chained half-glasses. She had a lilting British accent that at once conveyed authority and benevolence. "Have you been to Disney World?" she asked, and my despondent "No!" was followed by a litany of the places we'd been and my failed attempts to reach the Magic Kingdom.

A good Samaritan had given our car a jump, and Dad hustled over to retrieve me. "Young man!" my British friend greeted him, "You simply must take your family to Disney World! You will love it!" My dad smiled uncomfortably and nodded, and we walked silently back to the running car.

As we got in, my dad picked up the map and tossed it into my lap, "Look up how to get there."

"Where?" I inquired in disbelief.

"Disney World," came his sighed reply.

CONTRIBUTORS

Katie Baker lives in beautiful upstate New York, is an avid runner, and gets inspiration for her stories by getting outside and observing the people and landscape around her. Her work has been published in *Adelaide Literary Magazine*, *TWJ Magazine*, and *Torrid Literature Journal*. You can find her writing workshop on Seekingprose.com.

Adam Berlin has written four novels: *Headlock* (Algonquin Books), *Belmondo Style* (St. Martin's), *The Number of Missing* (Spuyten Duyvil), and *Both Members of the Club* (Texas Review Press). He teaches writing at John Jay College /CUNY and co-edits the litmag *J Journal*. Website: http://adamberlin.com. Twitter: @AdamBerlinNYC.

Robert Beveridge (he/him) makes noise (xterminal.bandcamp.com) and writes poetry in Akron, OH. Recent appearances in *Cerasus*, *Discretionary Love*, and *Sein und werden*, among others.

Barbara Bottner has written three YA novels, including the free verse *I Am Here Now*, 2020, as well as 50 books for children of all ages. She's published stories in *Cosmopolitan*, *Playgirl*, and various literary magazines. She's written essays for the *LA Weekly*, the *Miami Herald*, and reviewed children's books for the *NY Sunday Times*.

Bill Brown currently lives in Chapel Hill, North Carolina. He is the editor of a personal zine of travel writing called *Dream Whip*. Now in its 15th edition, it is published by Microcosm Publishing. You can also find a clutch of his travel stories on Matador Network: https://matadornetwork.com/author/billbrown/.

Jeff Burt lives in Santa Cruz County, California. He has contributed work to *Gold Man Review*, *Per Contra*, *Bird's Thumb*, and previously to *Lowestoft Chronicle*.

Lorraine Caputo is a wandering troubadour whose works appears in over 300 journals on six continents, and 23 collections of poetry—including *In the Jaguar Valley* (dancing girl press, 2023), *On Galápagos Shores* (dancing girl press, 2019) and *Caribbean Interludes* (Origami Poems Project, 2022). She also authors travel narratives, articles and guidebooks. Her writing has been honored by the Parliamentary Poet Laureate of Canada (2011) and nominated for the Best of the Net. Caputo has done literary readings from Alaska to the Patagonia. She journeys through Latin America with her faithful knapsack Rocinante, listening to the voices of the pueblos and Earth. Follow her adventures at www.facebook.com/lorrainecaputo.wanderer or https://latinamericawanderer.wordpress.com.

Jim Daniels' first book of nonfiction, *The Abridged Book of Water*, is forthcoming from Cornerstone Press. His latest book, *The Luck of the Fall, fiction*, was published by Michigan State University Press. Recent poetry books include *The Human Engine at Dawn*, Wolfson Press, and *Gun/Shy*, Wayne State University Press. His chapbook, *Comment Card*, Carnegie Mellon University Press, was published in 2024. A native of Detroit, he currently lives in Pittsburgh and teaches in the Alma College low-residency MFA program.

Kathy Dunkerley has worked as a magazine editor and journalist, and later as a Psychology Lecturer at Bristol University. She recently completed her first work of historical fiction and is writing her second book, which is a mystery novel that takes place in contemporary times. Her memoir of her travels in the Far East was previously published by the *Lowestoft Chronicle*.

Kathy is American but has lived in the UK with her family for over 40 years.

Jane Elkin is a language teacher, singer, and graphologist, inspired by a long memory for minutiae. She is the author of one chapbook, *World Class: Poems Inspired by the ESL Classroom*, and over a hundred other works of prose and poetry appearing in such publications as *Ruminate*, *The Best of Ducts.com*, *The Old Farmer's Almanac*, *Popula*, and *Angle*. The working title for her major work-in-progress is *Mother's Ink: A Momoir in Handwriting Analysis*. To learn more, visit www.jcelkin.net.

James Gallant was the winner of 2019 Schaffner Press Prize for music-in-literature for his story collection, *La Leona*, and *Other Guitar Stories*, published in 2020. *Fortnightly Review* (UK) published in 2018 in its Odd Volumes series a collection of his essays and short fiction, *Verisimilitudes: Essays and Approximations*.

David Hagerty is the author of the Duncan Cochrane mystery series, which chronicles crime and dirty politics in Chicago during his childhood. Real events inspired all four novels, including the murder of a politician's daughter six weeks before election day and a series of sniper killings in the city's most notorious housing project. He has also published more than 30 short stories, including many about his penchant for outdoor adventure. When he's not inventing disaster fantasies, he hikes, paddles, bikes, swims and skis. Read more of his work at https://davidhagerty.net.

C.B. Heinemann has been performing, recording, and touring with rock and Irish music groups for more than 30 years. *The Washington Post* said his songs are "...among the best coming from either side of the Atlantic," and *Dirty Linen* called him a "virtuoso." His short stories have appeared in *Florida English Journal*, *Berkeley Fiction Review*, *Chariton Review*, *Cigale Literary Magazine*, *Rathalla*

Review, Howl, Ascent, Lowestoft Chronicle, Outside In Literary & Travel Magazine, Storyteller, One Million Stories Creative Writing Project, The Whistling Fire, Danse Macabre, The Battered Suitcase, Fate, The Washington Post, Boston Globe, The Philadelphia Inquirer, Cool Traveler, Pittsburgh Post-Gazette, and *Road & Travel Magazine*. His stories have been featured in anthologies published by *Florida English Journal*, One Million Stories Creative Writing Project, and *Outside In Literary & Travel Magazine*.

Charles Holdefer, author of six novels, including *Don't Look at Me, Bring Me the Head of Mr. Boots, Magic Even You Can Do: By Blast*, and *Dick Cheney in Shorts, The Contractor*, and *Back in the Game*, grew up in Iowa and is a graduate of the Iowa Writers' Workshop and the Sorbonne. He currently teaches at the University of Poitiers, France. His short fiction has appeared in many magazines, including the *New England Review, Chicago Quarterly Review, North American Review, Los Angeles Review, Slice,* and *Yellow Silk*. His story "The Raptor" won a Pushcart Prize. He also writes essays and reviews which have appeared in *The Antioch Review, World Literature Today, New England Review, The Dactyl Review, The Collagist, l'Oeil du Spectateur, New York Journal of Books, Journal of the Short Story in English*, and elsewhere.

Ann Howells edited *Illya's Honey* for eighteen years. Recent books are: *So Long As We Speak Their Names* (Kelsay Books, 2019) and *Painting the Pinwheel Sky* (Assure Press, 2020). Chapbooks include: *Black Crow in Flight*, Editor's Choice in Main Street Rag's 2007 competition and *Softly Beating Wings*, 2017 William D. Barney Chapbook Competition winner (Blackbead Books).

Mark Jacobs has published more than 190 stories in magazines including *The Hudson Review, The Atlantic, Playboy*, and *The Baffler*. His sixth book, *Silent Light*, a novel set in the Congo, was published recently by Evergreen Review Books.

Mary Kreienkamp never quit her day job as an IT professional. She writes short stories at night for the entertainment of friends and family. Her pride and joy are her six nieces and nephews, for whom she serves as a cautionary tale.

Nicholas Litchfield is the author of the novels *Swampjack Virus* and *When The Actor Inspired Chaos and Bloodshed*. His stories, essays, and book reviews appear in *BULL, Colorado Review, Daily Press, Pennsylvania Literary Journal, The MacGuffin, The Virginian-Pilot, Washington Square Review,* and elsewhere. He has contributed introductions to twenty Stark House Press reprints of long-forgotten mystery novels. Formerly a book critic for the *Lancashire Post*, syndicated to twenty-five newspapers across the U.K., he now writes for *Publishers Weekly*. Reach him at nicholaslitchfield.com.

William Miller is the author of twelve award-winning children's books, a mystery novel, and eight collections of poetry. His most recent poetry collection is *The Crow Flew Between Us* (Kelsay Books, 2019). His poems have appeared in *The Penn Review, The Southern Review, Shenandoah, Prairie Schooner, West Branch,* and *Folio*. He lives and writes in the French Quarter of New Orleans.

George Moore's collections include *Children's Drawings of the Universe* (Salmon Poetry 2015) and *Saint Agnes Outside the Walls* (FutureCycle 2016). His poetry has been published in *The Atlantic, Poetry, Valparaiso, Stand, Orbis, Lowestoft Chronicle,* and the *Colorado Review*. He lives with his wife, a Canadian poet, on the south shore of Nova Scotia.

Tim Morris teaches English at the University of Texas at Arlington. His essays have appeared in *Raritan, Southwest Review, Gastronomica, The Decadent Review, Glacial Hills Review,* and *The American Scholar*.

Diana Senechal is the 2011 winner of the Hiett Prize in the Humanities and the author of two books of nonfiction, *Republic of Noise* (2012) and *Mind over Memes* (2018), as well as numerous poems, stories, essays, and translations. Her translations of Tomas Venclova's poems appear in his collections *Winter Dialogue* (1997), *The Junction* (2008), and a forthcoming volume; her translation of Gyula Jenei's collection *Mindig más* (*Always Different: Poems of Memory*) was published in 2022 by Deep Vellum. She has been living and teaching in Hungary since 2017.

A recovering economics professor, **Steve Slavin** earns a living writing math and economics books. Five volumes of his short stories have been published over the last six years, but he expects that the pace will slow.

Elizabeth Sowden is the author of *Tough Love at Mystic Bay*, a novel that takes on the troubled teen industry. She studied writing at Sarah Lawrence College. She lives in Minneapolis, where she enjoys martial arts, horses, and cooking.

K.C. Wolfe's essays, articles and short stories have appeared in *Gulf Coast, The Sun, Harvard Review, phoebe, Joyland, The Bark, Redivider, Under the Sun, Swink,* and other journals. Wolfe has worked as the associate nonfiction editor at *The Journal,* as a freelancer and as a managing editor. In 2007, he co-founded the literary journal *Sweet* and now serves as books editor and vice-president of the board of directors. He teaches in Eckerd College's creative writing program and lives, on average, in St. Petersburg.

Lee Clark Zumpe, an entertainment editor with Tampa Bay Newspapers, earned his bachelor's in English at the University of South Florida. He began writing poetry and fiction in the early 1990s. His work has regularly appeared in a variety of literary journals and genre magazines over the last two decades. Publication credits include *Tiferet, Zillah, The Ugly Tree, Modern Drunkard Magazine, Red Owl, Jones Av., Main Street Rag, Space & Time, Mythic Delirium*, and *Weird Tales*. Lee lives on the west coast of Florida with his wife and daughter. Visit www.leeclarkzumpe.com.

COPYRIGHT NOTES

Bon Voyage!

Intrepid Travelers

"Without a single stinker or filler piece in the bunch. I was extremely impressed with the variety and quality of the writing. *Intrepid Travelers* is a solid collection of funny and fine travel-themed stories, poetry, essays and interviews that easily fits in a back pocket or carry-on bag."
—FRANK MUNDO, Examiner.com

"Refreshing and well-written, Intrepid Travelers takes the reader to a wide variety of literary destinations, and makes even a confirmed hermit like me want to get up and go somewhere. Highly recommended."
—JAMES REASONER, *Rough Edges*

"Prepare for an adrenalin surge as a thief tries to escape from armed Mafia agents in Hector S. Koburn's fatalistic 'Bloody Driving Gloves,' Steve Gronert Ellerhoff's brilliantly quirky short story, 'Apophallation,' [and] Michael C. Keith's unexpectedly moving 'Pájaro Diablo.' *Intrepid Travelers* is a coruscating cornucopia of humour, drama and big, beautiful adventures. Highly original and entertaining."
—PAM NORFOLK, *Blackpool Gazette*

A Place to Pause

Edited by NICHOLAS LITCHFIELD
Foreword by Mary Donaldson-Evans

"A wonderful collection. Anyone who loves travel writing, or just plain good writing, will enjoy the variety of voices and situations chronicled here. Fresh, original, unpretentious, these writers and their work take us to a surprising number of physical and emotional places. A pure delight."
—JIM DANIELS, award–winning author of *Places/Everyone* and *Birth Marks*

"*A Place to Pause* is a delightful blend of captivating stories that inspired me to step away from my desk and experience all the vast glories beyond our screens."—Brian Sacca, actor and screenwriter of *Buffaloed*

"The collection is evenly split between poetry, fiction, and creative nonfiction, with three interviews with authors added for background…[and] delivers a certain uniformity in tone. Creative variations on a theme that often makes for vibrant reading."—*Kirkus Reviews*

To order, visit www.lowestoftchronicle.com

Other Places

"In the age of tweets and sound bites, it's heartening to read *Other Places*, a publication celebrating the power and beauty of a story well told."
—SHELDON RUSSELL, acclaimed author of the Hook Runyon Mystery series

"*Other Places*, a mouth-watering feast of short stories, poems, narrative non-fiction, and in-depth interviews, is the latest anthology from the much-admired *Lowestoft Chronicle*, an eclectic and innovative online journal. Packed into the pages are stories to entice, enthral, and entertain. Litchfield also serves up a tasty blend of pleasing and deftly prepared poems. And if you still aren't sated by this literary banquet, tuck into Litchfield's incisive and enlightening interviews with three critically acclaimed, multitalented writers."
—PAM NORFOLK, *Wigan Evening Post*

"I really loved the latest anthology from *Lowestoft*, *Other Places*. It's a brilliant, savory, sharp, amusing and varied taste of my favorite magazine, *Lowestoft Chronicle*. I'm delighted that a place exists for this kind of travel writing. This is just great writing about place, ranging from the spirit of place to the human spirit."
—JAY PARINI, internationally bestselling author of *The Passages of H.M.*

"*Other Places* is the usual delightful mix of stories, poems, author interviews, and non-fiction gleaned from the pages of the *Lowestoft Chronicle*, the only literary magazine I read on a regular basis. Always entertaining and insightful, *Other Places* is well worth your time, whether you're a veteran traveler or a hermit like me!" —JAMES REASONER, *New York Times* bestselling author

"Armchair travelers, rejoice! Editor Nicholas Litchfield has released *Lowestoft Chronicle*'s anthology for summer 2015, *Other Places*. The stories and poems vary in tone from dead serious to delightful whimsy, offering something for every taste. Humor, adventure and mystery share the pages with intriguing result."
—MARY BETH MAGEE, Examiner.com

"Whether humorous, touching, or revelatory, these expertly curated pieces throw you in contact with the real."
—SCOTT DOMINIC CARPENTER, author of *Theory of Remainders*

To order, visit www.lowestoftchronicle.com

The Vicarious Traveler

Edited by NICHOLAS LITCHFIELD
Foreword by Michael C. Keith

"I savored every locale. From the richly drawn desolation of the Texas panhandle in Sharon Frame Gay's "Song of the Highway" to the lush, bird-teeming lawns of "The Buzzing" by Philip Barbara; from the American nostalgia of "Mr. O'Brien's Last Soliloquy" by Robert Garner McBrearty to the Turkish apple orchard of Dave Gregory, this collection abounds with amazing language, arresting insight, and sharply drawn landscapes."
—LINDA BOROFF, screenwriter of *Murder in Fashion*

"Charm, a love of travel, often sly humor, and a clear reverence of story make up the backbone of *Lowestoft Chronicle*."
—KEITH ROSSON, acclaimed author of *Fever House* and *Smoke City*

"*The Vicarious Traveler* is a welcome travel-themed anthology that has something for everyone—adventure, crime, and humor all served up in sparkling prose and poetry."
—TIMOTHY J. LOCKHART, acclaimed author of *Smith*

An Adventurous Spirit

Edited by NICHOLAS LITCHFIELD
Foreword by James B. Nicola

"An amusing anthology of writing about travel. Among the many standout works is Tim Frank's "Three Strikes," whose premise is inventively and uncomfortably dark, and readers will savor its devilish twist. Meanwhile, poems such as "Woman With the Red Carry-On" are drolly perceptive."
—KIRKUS REVIEWS

"This anthology is a wideranging showcase of *Lowestoft Chronicle*'s writers, and the reader cannot help but be changed by this collective force."
—CAT DIXON, *The Good Life Review* Poetry Editor

"*An Adventurous Spirit* moves deftly, displays a remarkable range, and reminds us why we crave travel literature. Read and enjoy!"
—CHARLES HOLDEFER, author of *The Contractor*

"A treasure trove of excellent writing. This volume lives up to its claim of spirited adventure... The poetry also is remarkable. This book is a great find."
—JULIA MCMICHAEL, *Seattle Book Review*